DEATH IN THE DRESSING ROOM

Also by Simon Brett

The Fethering mysteries

BONES UNDER THE BEACH HUT
GUNS IN THE GALLERY *
THE CORPSE ON THE COURT *
THE STRANGLING ON THE STAGE *
THE TOMB IN TURKEY *
THE KILLING IN THE CAFÉ *
THE LIAR IN THE LIBRARY *
THE KILLER IN THE CHOIR *
GUILT AT THE GARAGE *
DEATH AND THE DECORATOR *

The Decluttering mysteries

THE CLUTTER CORPSE *
WASTE OF A LIFE *
A MESSY MURDER *

The Mrs Pargeter mysteries

MRS PARGETER'S PACKAGE
MRS PARGETER'S POUND OF FLESH
MRS PARGETER'S PLOT
MRS PARGETER'S POINT OF HONOUR
MRS PARGETER'S PRINCIPLE *
MRS PARGETER'S PUBLIC RELATIONS *
MRS PARGETER'S PATIO *

The Charles Paris theatrical series

SITUATION TRAGEDY *
MURDER UNPROMPTED *
MURDER IN THE TITLE *
NOT DEAD, ONLY RESTING *
DEAD GIVEAWAY *
WHAT BLOODY MAN IS THAT? *
A SERIES OF MURDERS *
CORPORATE BODIES *
A RECONSTRUCTED CORPSE *
SICKEN AND SO DIE *
DEAD ROOM FARCE *
A DECENT INTERVAL *
THE CINDERELLA KILLER *
A DEADLY HABIT *

* available from Severn House

DEATH IN THE DRESSING ROOM

Simon Brett

SEVERN
HOUSE

First world edition published in Great Britain and the USA in 2025
by Severn House, an imprint of Canongate Books Ltd,
14 High Street, Edinburgh EH1 1TE.

severnhouse.com

Copyright © Simon Brett, 2025

Cover and jacket design by Piers Tilbury

All rights reserved including the right of reproduction in whole or in part in any
form. The right of Simon Brett to be identified as the author of this work has been
asserted in accordance with the Copyright, Designs & Patents Act 1988.

British Library Cataloguing-in-Publication Data
A CIP catalogue record for this title is available from the British Library.

ISBN-13: 978-1-4483-1465-2 (cased)
ISBN-13: 978-1-4483-1466-9 (e-book)

This is a work of fiction. Names, characters, places and incidents are either the
product of the author's imagination or are used fictitiously. Except where actual
historical events and characters are being described for the storyline of this novel,
all situations in this publication are fictitious and any resemblance to actual
persons, living or dead, business establishments, events or locales is purely
coincidental.

All Severn House titles are printed on acid-free paper.

Typeset by Palimpsest Book Production Ltd.,
Falkirk, Stirlingshire, Scotland.
Printed and bound in Great Britain by TJ Books,
Padstow, Cornwall.

Praise for the Fethering mysteries

"An edgy cozy, filled with dry wit and deft plot twists"
Booklist Starred Review of *Death and the Decorator*

"A plot full of surprising twists and amusing detours. This is sprightly good fun"
Publishers Weekly on *Death and the Decorator*

"Brett is brilliant"
Booklist Starred Review of *Guilt at the Garage*

"Slyly witty . . . Well-developed subplots support the intricate narrative. Brett proves once again to be a master of the amateur sleuth genre"
Publishers Weekly on *Guilt at the Garage*

"Ingeniously drawn characters, deft timing of twists, and a to-die-for climax. A stunner"
Booklist Starred Review of *The Killer in the Choir*

"Peppered with wry wit, the story unfurls smoothly and swiftly"
Publishers Weekly on *The Killer in the Choir*

About the author

Simon Brett worked as a producer in radio and television before taking up writing full-time. He is the author of more than 100 books, including the much-loved Fethering mysteries, the Mrs Pargeter novels and the Charles Paris detective series, as well as the Decluttering mysteries. In 2014, he was awarded the Crime Writers' Association's prestigious Diamond Dagger for sustained excellence and contribution to crime writing, and in the 2016 New Year's Honours he was awarded an OBE 'for services to literature'.

Married with three grown-up children, six grandchildren and a ginger cat called Douglas, he lives in an Agatha Christie-style village on the South Downs.

www.simonbrett.com

To Janet, Pippa and Amanda,
with thanks

ONE

'But theatre people are so unnatural,' objected Carole.
'And how many "theatre people" do you know?' asked Jude.
'That's not the point.'
'I would have thought it was exactly the point. If you're going to condemn a whole profession in one sweeping generalization, I'm justified in asking on what research you base your findings.'
'Oh, you're so picky,' said an exasperated Carole. A remark in which there was a strong element of pot-and-kettle calling.

It was late February. They were sitting in the hygienic austerity of Carole Seddon's kitchen, drinking coffee from mugs. Her house was called High Tor, though there was nothing even vaguely like a high tor for nearly two hundred miles. Had Jude not lived right next door in Woodside Cottage and been the nearest Carole had to a best friend, the coffee would have been served in bone china cups and saucers in the sitting room. Carole had standards, and using mugs in the kitchen was about as close as she ever got to letting her hair down.

The kitchen may not have been welcoming, but at least it was warm. By the Aga, Carole's Labrador, Gulliver, snuffled contentedly in his doggy dreams.

The conversation that morning had been started by Jude saying she was going to the theatre on the following Saturday.
'So, what is it you're going to see?' Carole asked.
'Show called *House/Home*.'
Carole shook her head. The title meant nothing to her.
'Based on the television series of the same name . . .?'
Another shake of the head. One of Carole's very characteristic shakes of the head that always manifested itself to suggest that something was unworthy of her attention.
'So, why are you going to see it, Jude?'
'Old chum of mine's in the cast.'

'Oh yes?' And that was one of Carole's equally characteristic 'Oh yes?'es. It combined disapproval with contempt. 'Who is he?'

When Jude spoke of an 'old chum', it never occurred to her neighbour that she might be referring to a woman friend. Jude's relationship history had been varied and chequered, but not nearly as varied and chequered in reality as it was in Carole's imagination.

'Would I know his name?' she asked.

'Drake Purslow?' Jude offered.

'Never heard of him,' said Carole with considerable satisfaction.

'We worked together way back.'

Jude's working life had been as varied and chequered as her relationship history. She'd mentioned to her neighbour that she had, at times, been a model, an actress and a restaurateur. Surely, thought Carole, there must be further episodes of employment yet to be revealed? Despite her burning interest in Jude's past, her neighbour never asked direct questions about it. By her idiosyncratic scale of values, demonstrations of curiosity were somehow demeaning.

Though she knew the answer, Carole asked, 'In the theatre, I assume?'

'Yes,' said Jude. 'In a production of *The Birthday Party*.'

Carole was conflicted. Her assertion that she had no interest in the theatre was at odds with her desire to display her knowledge. Like the over-eager schoolgirl she had once been, with her hand always up because she knew the answer, she couldn't resist the urge to say, 'Pinter.'

'I played Lulu. Drake was Stanley. Long time ago.'

'And have you kept in touch with him since?'

'Hardly at all. I just saw his name in the Clincham Theatre winter brochure, thought it would be nice to say hello, and contacted him.'

'How did you do that?' asked Carole suspiciously.

'Rang the theatre. Left a message with the stage door keeper,' said Jude, beginning to weary of this interrogation. 'Drake rang me back.'

'I see,' said Carole. And she could put at least as much ominous implication into an 'I see' as she could into an 'Oh yes'.

Carole's ineradicable view remained that whenever Jude mentioned a man from her past, she was talking about an ex-lover. Or even, come to that, a current lover.

Where the pair lived, in the West Sussex seaside village of Fethering, there were two major theatrical venues within a forty-minute drive. To the east, in Brighton, was the magnificent nineteenth-century Theatre Royal, which featured pre- and post-West End plays and musicals, along with a mix of one-nighters by stand-up comedians and tribute bands. To the west was Clincham, whose 1960s theatre produced its own season of revivals and new plays during the summer season. From October to the end of May, it acted as a 'receiving house' for touring shows.

It was to Clincham Theatre that Jude was bound that weekend. There had recently been a vogue for reviving old television shows in stage versions. Producers, always on the lookout for cheap ways of making money, had grown more and more pussyfooted about funding new work. Increasingly, they relied on shows which already had name recognition. That is why the West End was littered with anodyne musicals based on successful movies. Give the public what they want. And the public, not being adventurous by nature, want things they've already heard of.

Following that principle, it had only been a matter of time before the producers moved from mining the cinema to mining television. For some years, rather than tackling whole plays, amateur dramatic societies had been putting on episodes of shows like *'Allo 'Allo!*, *Dad's Army* and *After Henry*. It was inevitable that that approach would soon move into commercial theatre. The arrival of *Fawlty Towers* in the West End was a manifestation of the trend.

The show that Jude was going to see that weekend was called *House/Home*, a title that would have been recognized by anyone who watched television during the late 1980s. The set-up was a group of provincial university students living in the same house, their activities monitored by the landlord, Mr Whiffen, who lived in the house next door with his redoubtable wife, Madeleine. Mr Whiffen was a technonerd, who kept trying to sort everything out on his primitive portable computer. This took a very long time to log on to, which led to Mr Whiffen's much-loved and much-quoted catchphrase, 'Let's just give it a minute, shall we?'

And Mr Whiffen had been played, from the start, by Jude's friend Drake Purslow.

The range of occupants in the rented house was different from what it would have been forty years later, in that there was not a single person of colour in the mix. Though from contrasting social backgrounds, they were all white. In order not to put off potential viewers who had no thought of ever going near a university, one of the housemates was not a student. Hayley, as she was called, worked on the checkout at a local supermarket. She was a salt-of-the-earth voice of reason, getting most laughs from her reactions to the aspirations and pretensions of the rest. Mr Whiffen and Madeleine were also from a lower class than most of their tenants.

The rest of the regular residents of the house included the toff, Edward, whose titled parents had always assumed he'd swan his way into Oxbridge. He prided himself on the 'common touch' he displayed with his housemates, unaware that they all regarded him as a buffoon.

The only one who engaged Edward in direct argument was Kieran, a robust Liverpudlian socialist, who interpreted anything that happened, anywhere in the world, as part of a conspiracy against the working class.

Belle was the beautiful one, so stunning that she prompted tongue-lolling male admiration even when she was munching cereal over the breakfast table. The irony was that her only interest was her academic subject of advanced mathematics and she was completely unaware of the effect she had on the opposite sex. There was a running joke throughout the series that, in spite of the rampant wishes of many young men to change that status, she might still be a virgin.

Then there was Angie, bosomy and blousy, bad at timekeeping and slovenly in dress, who had this amazing sex life. Much humour in the series derived from the varied specimens of masculinity who emerged from her bedroom in the late mornings.

Last was Spike, the eternal aspirant, always following some new lifestyle system which he was sure would change his prospects forever. He was eternally gullible and, in spite of constant disappointments, convinced every time that the next fad he adopted would be the one to really sort him out.

Most of the humour in the series derived from the disasters of the housemates' dating adventures and the large gap between their aspirations and their achievements.

In common with most television, *House/Home* was an amalgam of influences from other shows. In the relationship between Mr Whiffen and his tenants, there was a bit of *Rising Damp* or even *George and Mildred*. Angie's nymphomania, along with many of the jokes about it, was a straight lift from various characters in the *Carry On* films. The university house set-up had its origins in *The Young Ones* from the 1980s. And the whole concept of a group of young people not doing a lot – and exchanging contrived lines while they did it – was a lot more successfully realized in *Friends*.

That was not, however, the way the writer of *House/Home* saw it. Tony Grover reckoned that the entire thing was his exclusive creation. The genius displayed in the lines he wrote was the foundation stone of the series' success. Only grudgingly would he admit that the actors added some additional sparkle to the brilliance of his words. Like most writers, he was more than a little paranoid, and when it came to the global triumph of *Friends*, he frequently implied that he had had the original idea, which had been stolen from him.

As, without television's largesse, his income dwindled, Tony Grover became increasingly crabby and suspicious. He was convinced that the reason *House/Home* wasn't repeated in the main schedules much after the turn of the century was a personal vendetta against him by the broadcasters. He didn't believe it when told that the programmes had been shelved because the computer technology looked dated. Nor when the lack of repeats was attributed to some of the sexist innuendo in the scripts having become unacceptable to the enhanced sensibilities of the 2000s. *House/Home*, he was convinced, had become a victim of wokery.

Tony Grover kept trying other kinds of writing, in the hope of matching the healthy income stream of the television days, but none proved very productive. Like many failing writers, he tried teaching writing, but that wasn't a success either. His tendency to fill his courses with rants against the literary establishment – not to mention his predilection for getting too close to young female participants – meant that he was rarely asked back.

He'd lost count of the number of applications for grants he'd made to the Royal Literary Fund and similar charities.

For these and many other reasons – mostly financial – Tony Grover was desperate for the stage version of *House/Home* to be a success. Most of the original television cast had been re-assembled and some of them were now big box office names.

It was Tony Grover's dream that all of his financial and reputational troubles would be solved when the show transferred and had a long run in the West End.

Jude's view, when the show came to an end on the Saturday night, was that its success would be limited. Tony Grover had made a rather uncomfortable updating of *House/Home*. Making allowances for the fact that the cast had aged, the men losing hair and the women gaining poundage, he had used the creaky device of the students returning for a university reunion to find that the property, still owned by Mr Whiffen and Madeleine, had been converted into an upmarket Airbnb.

This enabled the characters to arrive in the present day and think back to various incidents that had occurred in their student days. These memories were then re-enacted in extracts from the original shows. This meant that there was no plot, just a kind of loosely linked Greatest Hits compilation. Jude wasn't convinced it worked.

Though you wouldn't have thought anyone shared that opinion from the enthusiasm expressed by the Clincham Theatre audience. She had gathered, from an overheard conversation between two of the front-of-house staff, that this was not only the last performance in Clincham but also the final performance of a tour that had been going on for three months, with a two-week break over Christmas.

Maybe that explained the audience hysteria at the curtain call. The last night of a tour might well be an occasion attended by partners, other family members and friends 'in the business', who had 'meant to catch up with the show earlier, but you know how it is, love . . .' Add to that list a bunch of ageing die-hard *House/Home* fans who'd followed all of the cast's doings since the series began, and you had the perfect recipe for audience ecstasy.

Which was, of course, expressed by a standing ovation. Jude, in a rare moment of old-fashionedness, was of the view that standing ovations were granted far too easily these days. Back when she'd been acting, such demonstrations of admiration had been rare, earned only by performances of exceptional brilliance. Whereas now, the ending of every tin-pot rip-off musical was awarded the accolade. Jude reflected that, maybe, the price they had paid for their tickets made every audience member determined to convince themselves that they had witnessed a rare moment of theatrical genius.

Anyway, the length of the applause and a riotous singalong from company and audience of the *House/Home* signature tune gave her a chance to slip out of her aisle seat and leave the auditorium before the crush.

She knew her way to the stage door. Though she'd never actually performed at Clincham Theatre, this wasn't the first time she had 'gone round' to see other friends in shows there. As she went back into the building, she heard the muted sound from the Tannoy of the riotous reception still going on onstage. The stage door area at Clincham Theatre had only two doors, the one through which Jude had entered from outside, and one opposite which led to the dressing rooms. Behind a counter, sitting in front of a row of empty key hooks and a cork board with cards pinned on it, sat a cheerful-looking woman, designed on the pattern of a (slightly deflated) beach ball.

'Evening,' she said.

'Hi. My name's Jude.'

'I'm Nell. Nell Griffin.'

'Hello. I've come to see Drake Purslow.'

'Don't know if he'll be there yet. All the cast are due to be having farewell drinks onstage.'

'Oh, shall I wait here?'

'No. Go on up and check. Dressing room seven.'

Drake Purslow was there.

He was lying on the floor, dead. There was an ugly wound on the front of his skull. Beside him on the floor lay a heavy, early portable computer. A gleam of fresh blood on its corner suggested a blow from that had killed him.

And, on the edge of the pool of blood, which had just stopped flowing, there was the small arc of a shoeprint.

TWO

Jude rushed back down the stairs. Nell looked up in surprise at her bursting through the interior door. 'What's the matter?' she asked.

'There's been an accident!'

The stage door keeper's hand was already reaching for a walkie-talkie on her desk. Theatre staff are well drilled in emergency procedures. 'Not another one,' she said, as she flicked the channel control. 'Is anyone badly hurt?'

'Yes. Drake.'

'Oh my God! What's happened to him?'

'It looks serious,' was all that Jude said. She certainly didn't mention the bloody shoeprint she'd seen. But that was very much on her mind. Of course, it could have belonged to someone who had walked into the dressing room and found Drake Purslow's body before she had. If that were the case, though, why hadn't they reported the discovery? The alternative explanation for the shoeprint was the one that appealed more to Jude's investigative instincts. That it had been left by Drake's murderer.

By now, Nell had got through on her call. 'Damn,' she said. 'She's not got her headphone switched on.'

But she was not fazed. She had other means of making contact. She changed the channel on the walkie-talkie, pressed a button and said, 'Could the nearest first-aider come to the stage door?'

He can't have been far away. He appeared almost immediately through the interior door. A man whose remaining hair was crinkled grey and whose face was heavily scarred from some old accident, maybe crashing through a car windscreen. He wore the stage crew uniform of dusty blacks. 'Yes, Nell?'

'Medical problem upstairs, Mo. Drake's dressing room.'

'OK. I'll check it out.' He didn't acknowledge Jude as he went back out through the door.

'Is he a paramedic?' she asked.

'Mo? No, he's part of the stage crew. But he's had training as a first-aider.'

'I see.'

It was not long before Mo was back in the stage door area. 'Looks pretty bad,' he said.

'Shall I call an ambulance?' asked Nell.

'No. Fee needs to know first.'

'She's not tuned in.'

'I'll go and get her,' said Mo, and disappeared back through the door.

Nell Griffin lifted the flap at the end of her counter and went to lock the stage door. 'Fiona Crampton's coming,' she explained to Jude. 'Theatre manager. She'll sort things out.' The confidence in her voice denoted the respect in which she held her superior.

'Just now,' said Jude, 'when I said there'd been an accident, you said, "Not another one." What did you mean?'

'Monday, during the tech run, the director had a stroke. He's in hospital.'

'Oh, I'm sorry. Who was—?'

Both women turned at the sound of tapping on the stage door. '*House/Home* fans,' said Nell. 'They'll have to wait. I'll do a notice.'

Again, she seemed to be going through a practised routine. She wrote on a blank sheet of A4, 'DUE TO A TECHNICAL PROBLEM, THE STAGE DOOR IS CURRENTLY LOCKED. PLEASE WAIT UNTIL THE ISSUE HAS BEEN RESOLVED.' This she stuck with Blu Tack to the inside of the window of the stage door.

By the time she'd done that, the theatre manager had emerged from the interior door. Mo was not with her, but as she came into the stage door area, a balding man in denim pushed his way after her, saying, 'Fiona, we haven't had a chance to talk.'

'Tony, can't you see I'm busy?'

'But you said we'd talk before the run ended.'

'Email me.'

'No. It's easier to ignore an email.'

'Tony—'

'Look. It's important to talk about the chances of a transfer.'

'I assure you that as soon as I have any news on that subject, you will be the first to know about it. Anyway, as you know, it's in the hands of the producers rather than Clincham Theatre.'

'But I—'

'Now will you please go back to the onstage party!'

By sheer force of personality – and a bit of brute force – the theatre manager got the man back through the door, which she then locked.

'Bloody writers!' she said. From which Jude deduced that the man in denim must have been Tony Grover, who, his self-penned biography in the programme told her, was the creator of the whole *House/Home* phenomenon.

The theatre manager turned towards her, and Nell made brief introductions. Jude found the only word to describe Fiona Crampton was 'neat'. She wore a smart bouclé suit that was predominantly pink and elegant flat shoes. Her blond hair was asymmetrically razor-cut tight to her head. The ensemble was perfect for someone whose work kept them continuously in the public eye.

The stage door keeper told her that Jude had discovered the body. 'How badly injured did you think he is?'

'I reckon he's dead.'

'That's what Mo said. I'd better have a look.' Fiona Crampton turned to Nell. 'I've told Ros, the stage manager' – she informed Jude – 'not to allow any of the company to leave the stage for the moment. There's no way we can stop the audience from leaving. And we can't keep the cast onstage for long. Because it's the last night of the tour, there are lots of partners and family members in the theatre.'

'But they'll have to come back to their dressing rooms soon. Wardrobe will be wanting to collect up their costumes.'

'I know, Nell.'

'Do you want me to call an ambulance?'

'Not yet. I'll have a look first.'

Fiona Crampton paused for a moment, maybe to gather herself for the unpleasantness ahead, and then started towards the dressing rooms.

She did not seem to mind that Jude and Nell went with her as she mounted the stairs. 'Drake would insist,' said the stage door keeper, 'on putting that crappy old computer up on a shelf. I told him it was dangerous . . . for him to keep lifting something as heavy as that – he wasn't a young man.'

In her flight, Jude had not closed Drake Purslow's dressing-room door. Mo had left it like that. The theatre manager stood in the doorway, with the other two women behind her, and looked in.

Nothing had changed from when Jude had discovered the body only moments before.

'Poor bugger,' said Nell. 'We should let Lazlo know, shouldn't we? Is he out front?'

'Lazlo – out front for a show he didn't direct?' Fiona Crampton spoke scornfully. 'The artistic director of Clincham Theatre actually on the premises? That'd be a rare sight.'

Jude recognized there was a whole backstory of office politics behind these comments, but it wasn't the moment to explore the subject.

'I'd better check for vital signs,' said the theatre manager.

With swift, economic movements, she snatched a bundle of tissues from the box on the shelf in front of the mirror, placed them on the edge of the pool of blood and knelt down. She had clearly had first-aid training. She found the carotid artery straight away and confirmed that there was no pulse.

As Fiona stood up, elegant as ever, Jude noticed that the bunch of tissues had been placed over the place where the arc of a shoeprint had been seen. Coincidence? Convenience? Or just a random accident of life?

Fiona brought up a number on her mobile. The fact that she had the emergency services in the memory suggested fatal accidents and other such incidents were all too common in the life of a theatre manager.

'Ambulance, please,' she said tersely into the phone. Then, after she'd been transferred, 'This is Fiona Crampton, manager at Clincham Theatre. We need an ambulance. There's been an accident to one of the actors in our current production.' She then replied to a series of routine questions.

One of her answers puzzled Jude. Clearly asked what condition the victim was in, Fiona Crampton replied, 'I don't know. He's not conscious, but I wouldn't say he was dead.'

She concluded the call and announced that the ambulance

would be at the stage door within ten minutes. 'I'll go back on-stage and find some reason why the cast can't go back to their dressing rooms yet.'

Then, reading some doubt in Jude's expression, she said, 'Do you have a problem?'

'I'm sorry. I just thought . . . You told them that Drake wasn't dead, whereas I think it's pretty clear that he is.'

'I'm not a doctor, am I?' said the theatre manager curtly, and went off down the stairs.

Sitting waiting by the stage door for the ambulance to arrive, Jude observed to Nell, 'Pretty primitive computer, wasn't it?'

'Yes, size of a sewing machine,' the stage door keeper agreed. 'And pretty much the same weight, too. The keyboard fits into the front of it like a kind of lid.'

'I didn't recognize the make.'

'You wouldn't. Apparently, there was a lot of legal toing and froing went on about the exact design. It was created specially for the television series. Needed to look like a real computer of the time, but not exactly like any existing model.'

'Oh?'

'Drake told me about it one evening when he came into the theatre early. The producers of *House/Home* didn't want to take the risk of using a real make of portable computer . . . though, apparently, quite a lot of the companies were keen to be featured . . . you know, "product placement" they call it, getting their goods in front of the viewers. Like BMX bikes in *E.T.*, if your memory goes back that far?'

'It certainly does.'

'Anyway, back then on *House/Home*, the computer companies suddenly got less keen on having their products featured when they discovered that one of the show's running gags was the fact that Mr Whiffen's portable computer was constantly breaking down.'

'Oh yes, of course.'

'Remember the catchphrase?'

Jude provided the answer, '"Let's just give it a minute, shall we?"'

'Yes, Drake still gets that shouted at him in the streets.' Nell

Griffin suddenly realized the change in the situation. 'Well . . . that is, he did.' Not wanting to linger on such uncomfortable truths, Nell went on, 'He told me the portable computer which they based the prop one on was called an "Osborne". Mean anything to you?'

Jude shook her head. 'Never heard of it.'

'Didn't last long. The company went belly-up in 1983. That's why the *House/Home* producers reckoned they could make Mr Whiffen's duff computer look a bit like an Osborne without fear of being sued. Apparently, Drake told me, the Osborne was one of the first computers to claim the name "portable", even though you had to plug it in wherever you'd carried it to. It was soon replaced by—'

Nell was interrupted by a phone ringing. Her responses told Jude the ambulance was announcing its imminent arrival. Fiona Crampton was summoned from the auditorium to greet the medical team.

Jude didn't have a car. She could drive and had driven much of her life, but in Fethering she didn't reckon she needed one. She had come to Clincham that evening by train and intended to go back the same way. But her planning ahead had not allowed for a dead body and the wait for an ambulance.

So, she rang the number of her secret taxi service. Jude was a professional healer, and many of the people in her life were former clients. Linton Braithwaite was one of them. He had had a serious problem with alcohol, but that was pretty much under control by the time he consulted Jude. His new challenge was how to fill the gaps in his life which used to be blotted out by the booze.

A few sessions in the front room of Woodside Cottage had changed his mindset. After disappointing a couple of wives during his drinking days, he now lived on his own. Money was not a problem. In spite of the booze, he had managed to build up a successful engineering company, whose sale put him in that enviable minority of people who can say they have 'enough money to last for the rest of my life'.

Much of his leisure time had been occupied by sport – mostly squash and tennis – and the heavy drinking sessions that followed.

But two knee replacements had put an end to that and left him with a lot of empty evenings, during which the temptation to slide off the wagon again was all too tempting.

This is a situation in which people are usually recommended to join a choir or take up bridge, but that wasn't the way Jude worked, and she knew such advice would be useless to Linton. Her healing was deeply idiosyncratic. Even when she was dealing with physical manifestations like allergic rashes or crippling back pain, she knew that what needed fixing was usually in the mind rather than the body.

Jude had been recommended to Linton Braithwaite by a female neighbour of his, whose excessive blushing problem she'd sorted out. The first time he'd arrived at Woodside Cottage, he'd been heavily marinated in scepticism. And yet he also wore the desperation of a man who had tried everything else and found that nothing had worked. And a man whose sleep patterns were deeply disturbed.

On that first occasion, Jude didn't frighten him by asking him to take any clothes off, but she did persuade him to lie on the treatment couch in her front room. Then, without actually making contact, she ran her hands up and down over the contours of his body, identifying the points of tension within it.

Jude had felt confident that she could do something to help him, but she wouldn't have been surprised if he had stomped off after that first session, muttering about 'charlatans' and even 'mumbo-jumbo'. That didn't happen. No, before leaving, he made another appointment.

Linton could not have described the effect Jude's ministrations had on him, and she herself would have had difficulty in saying why they worked. When she was healing, instinct took over. Some communion was established between her hands and the body beneath them.

It was she who suggested that he should become an after-dark taxi service, and Linton had quickly warmed to the idea. He didn't need the money, but he did need something to fill his empty evenings. And since he was likely to be awake anyway, driving someone to Gatwick for an early-morning flight made a lot more sense than tossing and turning under his duvet in search of that elusive sleep.

Also, the possibility of being called out by a client stopped him from even thinking about having a drink.

Having a practical mind, he quickly sorted out the required licences to make his business legitimate and was soon up and running. He didn't advertise his services; all his custom came by word of mouth. Since that word of mouth was spread initially by Jude, pretty soon most of Fethering knew about Linton Braithwaite's night taxi service.

And it was surprising how many people along the South Coast, apart from airport runs, needed rescue after missing last trains or sleeping through the station where they should have got off, how many teenagers having stayed too late at parties needed returning to their wrathful parents, and how many drunks saw sense and decided to leave their vehicles in the pub car park, to be collected the following day.

The lack of advertisement or online presence was not why Jude thought of Linton's as a 'secret' service. That was because it was secret from Carole. The owner of High Tor owned an immaculate white Renault, which resided in her unfeasibly tidy garage. On their investigative excursions, Carole frequently drove her neighbour. And was always ready with offers of lifts.

Though appreciative of these generous gestures, Jude was also aware of the hidden agenda behind them. Carole constantly claimed to have 'no interest in the minutiae of other people's lives' but was in fact almost pathologically nosy. And offers of driving her to places might reveal some of the 'minutiae' of her neighbour's social doings. Though habitually honest and open, Jude had certain compartments of her life that she kept closed. And she wanted them to stay that way.

One of the benefits Linton Braithwaite gained from his new employment was meeting a cross-section of people. He found himself becoming something of a psychologist, as he listened to conversations between passengers in the back seat or to the outpourings of garrulous ones in the front seat, desperate to unburden themselves to him.

He also knew instinctively when what was required of him was silence. And, having spent a lot of time with Jude, he detected that, that evening, she wanted to be quiet.

* * *

Sitting in the darkness at the back of the car, Jude thought about the scenes she had just witnessed at Clincham Theatre. Though still in shock, she could now begin to analyse the sequence of events. And the one thing that still struck her as odd was that Fiona Crampton hadn't checked whether or not Drake Purslow was dead.

'I'm not a doctor, am I?' The words resonated in Jude's mind. Well, it was undeniably true. The theatre manager was a theatre manager and not a doctor. But then she'd implied to the emergency services that the victim might still be alive.

Was that, possibly, thought Jude, so that an ambulance would arrive and take the body off theatre premises? Rather than the police being summoned to the theatre to start investigations into a suspicious death?

She wouldn't have thought of Drake Purslow's death as suspicious if she hadn't seen the bloody footprint Fiona Crampton had so conveniently erased.

THREE

'Why on earth would I want to watch a 1980s sitcom?' asked Carole on the Sunday evening. She was very wary about discussing her television viewing. Her parents had had strict opinions on the subject. Lord Reith had famously stated that the BBC's mission was to 'educate, inform and entertain'. They went along with the first two of those, but not the third. Carole's parents were happy to see their daughter watching news bulletins and wildlife documentaries, but the sound of a studio audience laughing was rarely heard in the house (though her father did make an exception whenever Tommy Cooper was on).

As with many of her inbred attitudes, this view of television had endured into Carole's adult life. She would admit to watching very little that wasn't factual . . . though she did have a guilty secret addiction to a drama series featuring a lot of nuns, wimples and placentas. But the idea of having been known to watch a sitcom was anathema to her.

'You might want to watch a 1980s sitcom,' said Jude patiently, 'because it would be research.'

'Research for what?'

'Research for a potential investigation.'

'Ah.' Now Jude had hooked her. Carole had an unquenchable thirst for a little light sleuthing. 'You're still thinking there was something fishy about your actor friend's death?'

Jude had mentioned some doubts to Carole on the Sunday after she'd been to Clincham Theatre.

'Something doesn't sit right in my mind.'

'Good,' said Carole, showing more enthusiasm than she usually allowed herself.

And then Jude mentioned the shoeprint. Which she knew she had seen, and which Fiona Crampton had so conveniently erased. A deliberate act? And if so, had it been done to hide a crime or simply to avoid a police investigation at Clincham Theatre? The theatre manager's single-minded devotion to the place made such a reading entirely believable.

'So,' Jude went on, 'I thought the first thing we should do is watch an episode of *House/Home*.'

'But where would you get it from?'

'Online. You can get virtually every television programme that's ever been made online these days.'

'If you say so.'

'I thought, Carole, that we could adjourn to Woodside Cottage, in whose front room I have a fire burning, and watch this episode of 1980s wackiness. Though, before we start, I will, of course, have opened a bottle of New Zealand Sauvignon Blanc.'

'That sounds very appealing.'

'Then you can bring your laptop and research what the various actors have been doing since the show finished.'

Carole looked thunderstruck. 'Bring . . . my . . . laptop?' she said haltingly.

'Yes.'

'But I keep my laptop in the office upstairs. In what used to be the spare room.'

'I know you do, Carole. But it is portable. That's the whole thing about laptops. They're designed to be carried wherever you go.'

'Yes, but, Jude, I do all my computer work up in my office,' Carole insisted feebly.

'Just go and get the bloody thing!'

And, with surprising meekness, Carole Seddon did what her neighbour told her to.

It was strange how much difference a few decades could make. The episode they watched was from the first series of *House/Home*, aired in 1986, and from the opening credits, it looked old-fashioned. Partly, that was because of the studio audience. Back then, Jude remembered a television director friend telling her, the conventional wisdom was that if you didn't have a studio audience, a show 'immediately dropped two million viewers'. That was, of course, before comedies like *The Office* demonstrated how effective a comedy programme could be without a laughter track.

As Carole and Jude watched in the comforting warmth of Woodside Cottage's front room, they heard a bouncy signature tune, accompanied by wild applause from an audience who had yet to see anything worth applauding. The title of the series swelled up in cartoonish bulk and vacated the screen for the episode title: 'NEW INTAKE by Tony Grover.'

Then the credits crossfaded into the setting of Mr and Mrs Whiffen's kitchen. It was a gloomy space, featuring a lot of cupboards in dark brown oak-effect wood. And it was shabby in the way television designers always overdo shabbiness. The message it meant to convey was that the Whiffens were scruffy and out of date, but nobody was quite as scruffy and out of date as the designer made them look. Television does squalor very well; it's less good at the kind of mild untidiness in which most people live. The *House/Home* kitchen dated from the 1950s.

The only 1980s contemporary object in sight was Mr Whiffen's famous computer, which, to avoid legal complications, was not called an Osborne, but which, with its lid opened to detach the keyboard, looked very much like an Osborne.

Because this was the first episode of a new sitcom, there was much setting up of the 'sit' before there could be much 'com'. Mr Whiffen and his wife Madeleine had to establish (a) that they were married, (b) that they owned the house next door which they let out to university students, and (c) that they didn't get on, because Mrs Whiffen was constantly suspicious of Mr Whiffen's 'outside interests'.

This was how Tony Grover, a competent but perhaps not the most subtle of television writers, answered the challenge:

> *Int. the Whiffens' kitchen. Day*
>
> *Mr Whiffen is working at his computer. Mrs Whiffen is reading a magazine. With satisfaction, Mr Whiffen presses a final key.*
>
> *Mr Whiffen:* There, Madeleine. I've got the names of all the new tenants on to the computer.
> *Madeleine:* And how long did that take you?
> *Mr Whiffen:* Matter of moments.

Madeleine [looking at her watch]: It took you fourteen minutes and twenty-three seconds. *[audience laughter]*
Mr Whiffen: Yes, well, I'm still learning to use the computer.
Madeleine: Huh. And how long did it take you to write down the list on the piece of paper that you then copied on to the computer?
Mr Whiffen: About the same, I would think.
Madeleine [looking at her watch]: It took you forty-seven seconds. *[audience laughter]*
Mr Whiffen: Ah. Well. Early days.
Madeleine: You've had that wretched machine for four months. *[audience laughter]*
Mr Whiffen: Rome wasn't built in a day.
Madeleine: No, but you can get lovely pasta there. Can your computer make pasta? *[audience laughter]*
Mr Whiffen: Not yet. It'll happen one day. The huge potential of computer technology has yet to be fulfilled.
Madeleine [with meaning]: I know how it feels. *[huge audience laughter]*

Jude stopped the recording. 'You get the idea,' she said.

'Yes, I do,' said Carole, her tone suggesting it was not an idea she wanted to get again in a hurry.

'OK, well, look up the actress who played Madeleine. Called Dani Simpkins. I've a feeling something unpleasant must have happened to her, because she wasn't playing the part in the stage version at Clincham Theatre.'

While Carole searched on her laptop, Jude shuffled through a pile of old newspapers and stuff on a stool by the fire. 'I think I've got the Clincham programme here somewhere.'

She felt relieved that, for once, her neighbour wasn't commenting on the clutter in her front room. Getting Carole interested in a case always diverted her from the usual litany of criticisms.

'I've found her,' said Carole, disproportionately triumphant. All she'd done was put the words 'Dani Simpkins' into Google. 'Oh yes, you're right.'

Jude leaned across to look at the screen. Carole didn't say anything, but the thought of someone else looking at her laptop troubled her. What she did upstairs in the spare room was private. It made her feel almost as bad as having someone peering over her shoulder while she did *The Times* crossword.

The Wikipedia article they both read about Dani Simpkins was brief. Or, at least, the relevant bit was. There was a long list of theatre credits and records of appearances in a slew of forgotten sitcoms, but the final paragraph answered their questions about her.

'She died in 2001 at the age of fifty-four. At the inquest into Simpkins' death, it was revealed that she had been drinking up to half a bottle of vodka a day for ten years, and recently very much more, and that she had become a victim of her own success, dreading the thought of being typecast as Madeleine Whiffen. The medical report stated that Simpkins' liver was twice the normal size and that her heart and lungs had also suffered because of her drinking; Simpkins' cause of death was given as portal cirrhosis of the liver. Friends suggested that she turned to drink to steady her nerves. Her situation degenerated after a divorce and subsequent failed relationships. She also suffered from loneliness, typecasting, scarcity of other work and lack of privacy due to the popularity of Madeleine Whiffen.'

'Tragic, really,' said Jude.

'Well, it sounds like she brought it on herself,' said Carole, predictably enough. She had an unfortunate habit of making remarks that sounded more callous than she meant them to be.

'Hmm . . .' said Jude. 'It's a cruel business, acting. You hear about the ones who make it big, but there are so many actors who just spiral off into nowhere.'

Carole was in no mood for reflections on mortality. 'Anyway, why are we bothering researching Dani Simpkins? She wasn't involved in the stage version of *House/Home* . . . for obvious reasons.'

'No. Useful to get the background, though.'

'Have you found that programme yet?' asked Carole testily.

'Yes.' Jude lifted it up.

'And who played Madeleine on the tour?'

Jude read the name. 'Ashley Maxted. There'll be a biog in here.'

But Carole was ahead of her. Before her neighbour had found

the relevant page in the programme, she had brought up the information on her screen. 'Hm. Doesn't warrant a Wikipedia entry. There's something on . . . IMDb?' The slowness expressed her lack of familiarity with the name.

Jude supplied the answer. '"Internet Movie Database". Lists every last detail about movies and telly programmes.' Instinct reminded Jude that Carole would rather she didn't look at the screen. 'Has Ashley Maxted got many credits?'

'Very few,' said Carole witheringly. 'Apparently, she played "Lauren" in *Harry's Hangover* and "Alien Princess" in *The Third Moon of Zimrod*.'

'Perhaps she did more work in the theatre?'

'Maybe.' Carole clicked a few more buttons. 'If so, there doesn't seem to be any record of it.'

'That's interesting,' said Jude.

'Why?'

'It's a nice part for someone without a great track record.'

'Suggesting what?'

'Suggesting that she might have been given the part because she was someone's friend.'

'Lover, you mean.'

'No, I don't mean "lover", Carole. Not every relationship between people in the theatre is physical.'

'Oh?' There were a few hundredweights of disbelief in the monosyllable. 'So, you mean one of the other actors might have been doing that Ashley Maxted a favour?'

'Possible. Or the director might be bolstering his position.'

'How do you mean – "bolstering his position"?'

'It's often the case that a director, facing the start of rehearsals with a cast he doesn't know well, will draft in actors he's worked with before – you know, so's he's got some people on his side from the start. And, with something like *House/Home*, where the cast have all known each other for decades, the case for doing that might be even stronger.'

Carole let out the sort of grunt favoured by people who will never understand the ways of theatricals. 'So, who is the director?'

Jude flicked through the programme. 'Ah. No,' she said, as she found the name. 'My theory doesn't work.'

'No?'

'It's the original director of the television series. Johnny Warburton. God, they must have got him out of retirement to do the stage show.'

Carole's fingers were already on the keyboard. 'Let's see what we can find out about him.'

'I wouldn't bother.'

'What?'

'If we're looking for the person who killed Drake Purslow, Johnny Warburton's off the list of suspects.'

'Oh?'

'He had a stroke last Monday. The stage door keeper told me. He's in hospital.'

'Oh . . .' Carole looked rather like a puppy whose bone has been taken away. 'So, if we can't research any more . . .'

'We'll watch a bit more of the show,' said Jude.

Int. communal kitchen. Day.

Edward and Kieran are sitting over the remains of a messy fry-up breakfast. The shot starts on the wall clock. The time is 11.45.

Kieran: But, Edward, how can you possibly justify private education?

Edward: Well, Kieran, me old mucker, it's based on a very simple principle that the more you pay for something, the better the quality of what you get.

Kieran: That doesn't work with footballers. *[audience laughter]*

Edward: Doesn't it?

Kieran: Have you seen the current Liverpool squad? *[audience laughter]*

Edward: Don't know much about soccer, I'm afraid. I've always favoured oval balls. *[audience laughter]*

Kieran: Really? *[audience laughter]* How come you don't surprise me, you blue-blooded buffoon! *[audience laughter]*

Edward: No, but seriously, Kieran . . . At Christmas lunch,

> wouldn't you prefer your father to be opening a vintage bottle of Bordeaux, rather than some cheap plonk? *[audience laughter]*
>
> *Kieran:* My Da wouldn't be there for Christmas lunch. He'd be down the docks doing an extra shift, so's he can buy a toy for my kid brother.
>
> *Edward:* Cor blimey! *[he mimes playing a violin.]* Bring on the violins. *[audience laughter]*
>
> *Kieran:* Dead right for you, that is.
>
> *Edward:* What do you mean?
>
> *Kieran:* You toffs are always on the fiddle. *[audience laughter]*
>
> *The kitchen door opens to admit a very tousled-looking Angie. She wears a dressing gown.*
>
> *Edward:* Ah, and here she is – Angie the unmade bed. *[audience laughter]* Just in time for the midday news.
>
> *Angie:* For students, the midday news is breakfast television. *[audience laughter]*
>
> *Kieran:* So, Angie, did you spend last night on your own?
>
> *Angie:* I'll spend a night on my own when the world runs out of men. *[audience laughter]*
>
> *Edward: [ruefully]* I've got women friends who can't wait for that moment to arrive. *[audience laughter]*
>
> *Angie:* Well, I'm not among them. Men are remarkably easy to deal with . . . if you're good with animals. *[audience laughter]*
>
> *A bewildered young man enters through the open door. He is very tall and handsome, dressed in just his boxer shorts and a sheet over his shoulders.*
>
> *Angie: [casually]* Oh, hi. This is Edward . . . and Kieran.
>
> *Edward and Kieran:* Hi.
>
> *Angie:* And this is . . . Sorry, I didn't get your name. *[audience laughter] [sexily]* Though I did get everything else. *[huge audience laughter and applause as the camera closes in on the wretched young man.]*

'Well, I don't think I missed anything, not seeing that first time round,' said Carole frostily, as she reached towards her laptop. In the course of their viewing, she had surreptitiously commandeered the *House/Home* programme and was keying in the first of the relevant names.

'Gerald Tarquin,' she said, 'who played Edward, doesn't seem to have done a lot more after the series ended. A few credits in the early 2000s, then nothing more.'

'Having seen him in the show on Saturday night,' said Jude, 'I can see why.'

'Oh?'

'He's just not a very good actor. And back in the telly series, of course, that didn't matter so much. He was very good-looking, and he had the right private-school accent. The character he was playing was pretty wooden, so he got away with it. Had a great following among teenage girls. But then he started to lose his hair and chubbied out a bit. And he walks with a limp – must've had some kind of accident, but it didn't add to his charms. He was the kind of actor who could only really play one part, and he no longer looked that part. You can see why the work started to dry up.'

'You seem to know an awful lot about him,' Carole observed suspiciously.

'No. I've just seen the same thing happen to lots of actors.'

'Hm.' Carole's fingers skittered over the keyboard before she announced, 'Todd Blacker, who played Kieran, seems to have been a lot busier.'

'Yes. In theatre, wasn't it?'

'Yes,' said Carole, a little miffed that her neighbour seemed already to know the stuff she was about to reveal. 'Founded some group called "Pig in a Poke Theatre".'

'Very experimental, as I recall. Famous for his impro techniques.'

'"Impro"?' Carole didn't know the word.

'"Improvisational".'

'Oh.'

'Didn't start off with a script. The cast spent weeks developing characters, which the director then knocked into a storyline.'

'Oh. Did you ever get involved in that kind of process when you were acting?'

'Only marginally. I always thought plays needed playwrights.

The impro approach was just an excuse for control-freak directors to indulge in a long ego trip.'

'Isn't it rather odd,' said Carole, 'that someone with such a taste for experimental theatre should go back to be in a stage version of a popular sitcom?'

'Nothing odd about it at all. Most actors are susceptible to a large pay packet.'

'Ah.'

'And, of course, Angie,' said Jude, moving through the cast list, 'was played by Babs Backshaw.'

'You say the name, Jude,' said Carole, 'as though I should have heard of her.'

'She is pretty hard to avoid these days.'

'Enlighten me,' said Carole, at the same time keying the name into her laptop.

'Babs Backshaw was the most successful one from *House/Home*. She got picked up on the chat show circuit. Became famous using four-letter words and talking about farting.'

'Oh,' said Carole, all middle-class disapproval.

'Then, for some reason, she got spotted by Hollywood. Hollywood always seems to have space for one fat actress who gets all the fat parts, and for a few years, Babs Backshaw was it. Millions of followers on social media. Now she's an authentic star. Damn near a national treasure. The sort of personality they send off to foreign countries to front documentaries called *Babs Backshaw's Sri Lanka* or whatever.'

'Yes, I've just found her on Wikipedia,' said Carole, transfixed by her screen. 'Not many of the cast of *House/Home* made it to Wikipedia. Goodness, she's been amazingly busy. And still only in her fifties. I wonder how she's fitted it all in.'

'Success breeds success. Become a recognized name and everyone wants a bit of you.'

'Do you ever wish your career had taken off like that, Jude?'

'Me? God, no.'

'You've never told me why you gave up acting.'

'That's true,' said Jude with a serene smile.

'In fact, there's still quite a lot you haven't told me about your past.'

'Yes,' Jude agreed, in a benign way that ruled out the possibility of Carole probing further. 'Babs Backshaw has had an amazing career. She seems to have done everything.'

'Including murdering Drake Purslow?' asked Carole.

All this showbiz detail was mildly interesting, but she knew where her real priority lay.

FOUR

Int. communal kitchen. day.

The breakfast detritus has been cleared away. Belle is sitting at the table, with a pile of textbooks, working out calculations in an exercise book. Spike is sitting on a chair away from the table, apparently reading a book, but really watching Belle with undisguised lust. Hayley enters, taking off her outdoor coat.

Hayley: Hi, Belle.
Belle: Hi, Hayley.
Hayley: Still doing your sums?
Belle: I prefer to think of it as advanced mathematics.
Hayley: I prefer to think of it as sums. *[audience laughter]* Actually, I prefer not to think about it at all. At school, there were two things I hated. Sums . . . and [WITH VENOM] Miss Pritchett. *[audience laughter]*
Belle: What did Miss Pritchett do to annoy you?
Hayley: She taught me sums. *[audience laughter]* Oh, hello, Spike. I didn't notice you.
Spike: No. That often happens to me with women. *[audience laughter]* Belle, do you notice me?
Belle [not hearing him and opening a book]: Page forty-seven, right. *[audience laughter]*
Spike [to Hayley]: See what I mean? *[audience laughter]*
Hayley [not hearing him]: Funny thing happened at the supermarket today.

Spike's face shows his frustration. [audience laughter]

Hayley: Pensioner comes to me at the till, holding a loaf of bread. She says, 'Is this all right for gluttons?' I say, 'Yes, if you eat enough of it.' *[audience laughter]* She says, ''Cause my daughter insists on the bread being glutton-free.' *[audience laughter]* And I say, 'Well, I don't know about the glutton bit, but it's certainly not free.' *[audience laughter]* I don't know. Some people . . .'

Jude pressed the stop button. 'That became her catchphrase.'

'I beg your pardon?' asked Carole.

'It didn't get much of a laugh there, because it was the first episode, and it hadn't caught on yet. But, as the series developed, the audience would be waiting for her to say the words. And it became the title for Linda Winket's spin-off series. *Some People . . .*'

'I'm sorry,' said Carole, with some hauteur, 'but I have no idea what you're talking about.'

Jude sighed. 'Let me explain. "Some people . . ." became the character Hayley's catchphrase. Impressionists started doing it. Kids shouted it at each other in school playgrounds. And "Oh, you blue-blooded buffoon!" – that was another one. Again, didn't get much of a laugh in the first episode, but later in the series, the audience would be waiting for Kieran to say the "buffoon" line to Edward, and then it'd get a huge laugh and round of applause.'

Jude looked at the blank incomprehension on her neighbour's face. 'You do know what a catchphrase is, don't you, Carole?'

'I have heard the expression.'

'It's things like "Stupid boy" from Captain Mainwaring in *Dad's Army*. Or "Suit you, Sir" from *The Fast Show*. They catch on.'

'Why?'

'They just do.'

'I'm sorry,' said Carole with dignified pride. 'I still have no idea what you're talking about.'

'Never mind,' said Jude, in some frustration. Sometimes Carole could be just . . . so . . . so . . . Carole.

'Anyway,' said Carole in a tone that suggested Jude had been distracting her from her serious purpose, 'I will check out Belle first. The beautiful one.' She looked in the programme. 'Played by Anita Harcourt.' Her fingers were busy on the keyboard. 'Ah. She started off as a model. *House/Home* was her first acting job.'

'That happens quite a lot.'

'Model to actress?'

'Yes.'

Eager to pounce on any clue about her neighbour's past, Carole asked, 'Did it happen to you?'

'In a way,' Jude was forced to concede.

Carole nodded with satisfaction at having elicited that tiny detail, but made no comment and returned her attention to the screen. 'Hm. Looks like *House/Home* was her only major acting job.'

'Really? I remember she was hugely popular. Lusted after by the entire masculine population. Photos of her on the walls of every male student bedroom in the country.'

'Well, from what it says here, she continued to do some acting and modelling until round 2000, and then completely dropped off the radar.'

'Strange.'

'If you don't believe me, have a look for yourself,' said Carole, spiky as ever.

'Of course I believe you. Just wondering what might have made her give it all up.'

'And what would have induced her to come back for the stage show.'

'Exactly.'

'Very different story for Linda Winket,' observed Carole. 'She merits Wikipedia, too. Acres of stuff.'

'Yes, she really came out as the star of *House/Home*. None of the others went on to have their own series.'

'*Some People* . . . ,' said Carole with distaste. She consulted the screen. 'And Linda Winket doesn't seem to have been out of work since.'

'No. She's just one of those personalities the British public love. Working-class, straight-talking, funny – often at her own expense. And clearly works hard. Singing, dancing, musicals . . . Married her boyfriend from school, had three kids, always got time to chat to everyone. It's hard to resent her success.'

Carole sniffed. She didn't, generally speaking, find resenting anything hard. 'Moving on to the boy, Spike . . .'

'Ollie Luke,' Jude supplied. 'Yes, sad story, his.'

'How do you know that?' asked Carole testily.

'Because I keep up with the news.'

'I keep up with the news, too.'

'Yes, but you're more interested in matters of international importance than the minutiae of showbiz lives.'

Carole regarded that as a compliment. Mollified, she said, 'Yes, you're probably right.'

Jude pointed to the programme. 'Look, at least they've acknowledged the deceased. It says, "This production is dedicated, with much love, to the memories of Dani Simpkins and Ollie Luke."'

Carole looked down at her screen. 'Ollie Luke died in the early nineties. Cause of death . . . a drug overdose.'

'There was quite a lot of press coverage at the time,' said Jude.

'Well, I didn't see any of it.'

'Evidently.'

Carole looked at her neighbour beadily. Maybe her last comment hadn't been as complimentary as the previous one had been.

'It was soon enough after the series for Ollie Luke still to be a popular figure. And he'd got some good television parts after *House/Home* ended. His death brought misery to a lot of teenage girls.'

'Pity there isn't more about how it happened.' Carole subjected her screen to a look of disappointment. 'Oh, I've just had a thought. If Ollie Luke died all those years ago, who played the part of Spike in the recent tour?'

Jude consulted the programme again. 'Will Quirke. Never heard of him.'

'Was he good in the play?'

'Not great. But very good-looking. Quite the heartthrob. Looks like he's new to the acting. Only credits listed here are for singing and dancing on cruise ships.'

'Nothing else about him?'

'Nope,' said Jude with finality. 'I'm sure we can find out more if we dig deeper.'

'Maybe . . .' Carole seemed to be losing her initial enthusiasm for the chase. 'Of course, it's entirely possible,' she said, 'that if your friend was murdered, the perpetrator might have had nothing to do with this *House/Home* programme.'

'I agree.' Jude sounded a little deflated, too. 'But I thought it was important that we should get a bit of background to the show.'

'Maybe . . .' Carole said again, unconvinced.

'First thing we need to do,' said Jude with renewed positivity, 'is to finish off this one' – she poured the remains of the New Zealand Sauvignon Blanc into the two glasses – 'and open another bottle.'

'Goodness. Have we really got through—?'

'Yes, Carole. We have.'

Jude did the business with the bottle. Which, given the fact that it was a screw-top, didn't present too much difficulty. She topped up the glasses and said, 'Come on, a toast to solving this murder.'

'If it is a murder,' said Carole subversively. But she did raise her glass and even echoed Jude's cry of 'To solving the murder!'

After they'd both taken a long swallow, Carole said, 'Of course, the one person I hardly know anything about – and you, I'm sure, know a great deal about – is the victim.'

'I don't know much about him. As I told you, I hadn't seen him for years.'

'Ah, but there was a time, wasn't there, when you were working together, that you were . . . very close?' Once Carole Seddon had got an idea in her head, it took a lot of dislodging.

As on many previous occasions, Jude didn't rise to the bait. 'Yes, but I don't know much about his life since those days. What can you find on him?'

Carole searched on. 'Oh, he qualifies for Wikipedia, too.'

'He did have quite a high profile at one time. Great things predicted for him as a classical actor. Worked at the National and the RSC.'

'Yes, there's screeds of stuff about that.'

'What does it say under "Personal Life"?'

'Do you want to know if you get a mention?'

Once again, Jude forbore to respond.

Carole found the relevant entry. 'Was married to someone called "Kirsten Loader". She's printed in blue, which means she's got her own Wikipedia entry.'

'Yes, she's an actress.'

'Surprise, surprise.'

'They were together when Drake and I did *The Birthday Party*.'

'Well, they're no longer together. Divorced way back. But . . . Drake Purslow is now said to have a "partner".'

'Really? Who's that?'

'She's also printed in blue. Imogen Wales.'

'Ah,' said Jude. 'I know her.'

Though the desire was unspoken, Jude knew that Carole desperately wanted to come with her. But that was never going to be possible. Imogen Wales was an old friend, though they hadn't met for some decades. But to visit the newly bereaved actress and take along a woman she'd never met before was out of the question.

Of course, Carole knew the logic of this, but she still gave a rather huffy greeting to her neighbour on the Monday morning. Jude had just emerged from Woodside Cottage, on her way to Fethering Station to catch the London train. And, by pure coincidence – maybe – Carole had just emerged from High Tor with Gulliver. 'Going to take him for a long walk on the beach. He needs more exercise when the weather's like this.'

'It should be pretty bracing down there.'

'Yes.' Carole feigned ignorance. 'And where are you off to?'

'London. To see Imogen Wales.'

'Oh yes, of course. I'd forgotten,' Carole lied.

'I'll report back this evening.'

'Oh yes, sure. If you want to.' A tug on his lead, and dog and owner were off towards Fethering Beach.

With a wry, inward grin, Jude set off for the station to catch the first off-peak train to London.

'The irony is,' said Imogen Wales, 'that Drake was a complete technophobe.'

Obviously, she had aged since Jude had last seen her in the flesh. But because of her ubiquity, appearances onstage, television and film, profiles in the arts pages of the press, the entire country had witnessed her ageing. And, in her sixties, Imogen Wales remained a very beautiful woman.

She was still whippet-thin and had never dyed her hair (except when a part required it). Its steel grey was cut in the same pageboy style as it had been when it was luxuriant chestnut. The cut emphasized her perfect jawline. She was simply dressed, in black trousers, black pumps and a dark grey silk shirt.

Her home was a third-floor mansion flat in Prince of Wales Drive, with extensive views over Battersea Park. Through the winter-stripped trees, there was even the occasional silver glint from the Thames. The flat's décor was expensive but understated. There were no photographs on display. Some actresses Jude had known lived surrounded by images of themselves in various roles. That was not Imogen Wales's style.

But style was something she very definitely had. Had had when Jude had first worked with her, when they were both making their way in 'the business'. From the moment she arrived on the theatrical scene, Imogen Wales was the complete package. She was also, Jude recollected, deeply serious about her acting. Serious to the exclusion of having any sense of humour.

'He was a Luddite at heart,' Imogen went on. 'It almost became a fetish with him. Drake didn't have a website, didn't do emails and certainly wouldn't go near social media. He could just about manage texting on his extremely unsmart phone. And for him, in death, to be forever associated with that wretched primitive computer . . . not to mention being associated with that dreadful sitcom . . . it doesn't bear thinking of.'

'But is it public knowledge what actually killed him? I've looked online, and all I've found so far is that he was "killed in a backstage accident".'

'It'll soon get out what actually happened.'

'Do you think so?'

'Jude, of course it will. Actors are the most gossipy people on God's earth. And they all spend their lives on social media, or just Googling for references to themselves. Some of the cast of that show at Clincham Theatre will know the circumstances of Drake's death. It's only a matter of time before it gets leaked to the press.'

'You're probably right.' Jude was nonplussed by Imogen Wales's calmness. Here she was, a woman whose partner had just been killed in what, at the very least, had been a nasty accident, and she was showing no signs of stress at all. Was she really as unaffected by the tragedy as she appeared to be?

Imogen seemed to read her thoughts, because she said, 'You must think I'm very callous, talking about Drake in this way.'

'No, of course not.' Though it was exactly what Jude had been thinking.

'The fact is, I haven't yet processed what's happened. All my focus is on the show.'

Oh damn, thought Jude, I should have checked online what Imogen Wales is working on at the moment. She had the feeling it was something in the theatre.

The actress confirmed this. 'I'm giving my Volumnia in *Coriolanus* at the Duke of York's.'

'Oh yes, I read about it,' said Jude. Which was almost true.

'And I'm afraid Volumnia is one of those parts that require an actor's complete focus. If I'm to give the performance the part demands, then I can't think about anything else.'

'No, I'm sure you can't,' said Jude. Though she could think of quite a few people – even actors – who would be able to shift their focus elsewhere. Particularly if their partner had just been murdered.

'Drake would fully understand,' said Imogen, as though once again reading Jude's mind. 'He would have behaved the same way, had the situation been reversed. He understood that to give one's best performance, one must not be distracted by extraneous thoughts. That's why, though Drake and I loved each other, we never lived together, always kept our separate flats. So that we could maintain our focus on the work.

'Not just that, of course. It was so that we were both open to the possibility of other lovers. Not serious ones, of course. Just flings. Light-hearted flings.' Jude couldn't imagine Imogen ever having done anything light-hearted in her life. 'Actors must be open to new experiences. Because it is the emotions we have experienced in our own lives that provide the reservoir of emotions that we draw on for the characters we create.'

Jude had heard similar justifications of promiscuity from many male actors. It was strange to hear the words coming from a woman's mouth. The seriousness with which they were spoken suggested to her that the male guinea pigs researched in Imogen Wales's bed might not have a very jolly time of it.

She wasn't about to express those opinions, but she wouldn't have had time anyway as Imogen went on, 'And, of course, because ours was such a balanced relationship, Drake always had exactly the same freedom to take lovers as I had.'

'I see,' was all Jude allowed herself by way of comment. 'As I said, it's a long time since I last saw Drake. But when I saw he was going to be appearing at Clincham Theatre . . . It seems it was fortunate that I contacted him by old-fashioned telephone, rather than email or WhatsApp or something like that.'

'You're absolutely right. His agent got very cross about it. When they needed to contact Drake, they'd email me.'

'Ah. Did you manage to see the *House/Home* stage show anywhere on the tour?'

'Good God, no!' The thin body shuddered, as if Jude had asked whether she indulged in a particularly obscene sexual practice. 'It was appalling, the shadow that series cast over Drake's career. I met him first when we were both starting out. And he was as serious about "the business" as I was.

'But most of us, at some point in our career, have to make choices about the work we choose to do. And when the offer for *House/Home* came through, Drake was married with small children, and the mortgage had to be paid.

'So, he took the job. Little knowing how much he would come to be defined by that wretched Mr Whiffen character. It took a long time for Drake to regain any credibility in the legitimate theatre world after that. He hated every minute he spent on *House/Home*.'

'Then why did he agree to do the tour?'

'Drake was a man of integrity. He would never let down his fellow artistes. When he found out how many of the old team were up for it, he couldn't be the one who let them down. And the dates fitted for him. He would just finish the tour before he started preparing for his next role. He was due to give his Gloucester in a new *Lear* at the Donmar. Would have been due to start rehearsals for that next Tuesday.'

For the first time, the realization of Drake Purslow's absence – from a theatrical commitment, obviously – seemed to threaten Imogen Wales's equilibrium.

But the moment soon passed. She turned her famously piercing blue eyes on her visitor. 'You said, when you contacted me, that you were the first person to discover Drake's body.'

'Yes.'

'And that terrible old computer, the prop from the television series, had accidentally fallen from a shelf on to his head?'

'That's what appeared to have happened, yes.'

Imogen immediately recognized the slight uncertainty in Jude's tone. 'Are you suggesting there might be another explanation?'

'Well . . .' Jude decided she might as well go for broke. 'The possibility did cross my mind . . . that if someone had wanted to murder Drake, then the perfect blunt instrument was there, sitting in his dressing room.'

'Yes.' Imogen was attracted by the idea and would have liked to pursue it, but her professional priorities prevented her from doing so. 'That's another idea I'll have to process after the *Coriolanus* run has ended.'

The actress glanced at her watch. Jude knew that soon she would announce that their conversation was beginning to spoil her concentration on the character of Volumnia. Having seen Imogen's interest in the murder scenario, she did not want to lose her attention too quickly. 'It's the corny old question that's appeared in every crime series since John Logie Baird invented television, but . . . did Drake Purslow have any enemies?'

'Few people can go through a theatrical career without putting a few backs up along the way.'

'Yes, but I meant more *focused* than that.' Jude liked throwing Imogen's own word back at her. 'Any major fallings-out?'

'Well, there were directors he wouldn't work with again. And some actors. Basically, the type of actors who larked around at rehearsals, you know, didn't take the work seriously enough.'

'But no individual with whom he had an ongoing conflict?'

'Don't think so . . .' But something had struck a chord. Imogen reached for her mobile phone and started searching through her records. 'This was a bit strange. As I said, if anyone wanted to email Drake, they tended to do it through me. Usually his agent, work things, you know.' She found what she was looking for. 'Came maybe a month ago. Drake pooh-poohed it, suggested some crank had sent the thing. He said the internet was full of cranks and loonies – another reason why he had nothing to do with it. But it was strange.'

Imogen Wales held the phone towards her visitor.

What Jude read on the screen was: *'You've got away with it for a long time, Drake Purslow. But there's going to be a time – in the not-too-distant future – when your sins will catch up with you.'*

FIVE

Carole had fully understood why she couldn't go with Jude to talk to Imogen Wales, but she could not deny that she felt a bit miffed at being excluded. An investigation – particularly a murder investigation – wrought strange changes in Carole Seddon's personality.

Though full of strong opinions, she did not usually wish to raise her head above the parapet. Inwardly seething was a much more natural state to her than making a public demonstration of her feelings. She would never have used the word about herself, but Carole was actually shy. Shy in a crowd, shy in particular about meeting new people. The intimidating attitude she presented to the world, which appeared to express a frosty lack of interest in the doings of others, in fact reflected the exact opposite.

But when there was a hint of an investigation on the horizon, her attitude changed completely. The 'demands of the case' became paramount. Her interest in the doings of others ceased to be Carole Seddon being nosy; it became a necessary part of the investigative process. And the demands of that justified any amount of social interaction, even to the extent of approaching people she did not know. Which, given the background of the case in question, might well include 'theatre people'.

What's more, after prolonged initial resistance to the whole business of computers, Carole now worshipped her laptop with the zeal of a convert. And whole wide vistas of online research had opened up to her.

The morning she'd seen Jude on her way to London, after giving Gulliver an exhaustive workout on Fethering Beach, Carole was straight on to her laptop. In its proper place, of course. The spare bedroom at High Tor, which was now her dedicated computer room. It still didn't feel right using the technology anywhere else.

Carole had now got quite good at accessing back numbers of newspapers and finding what she wanted. She had been helped in this skill by a former journalist on the *Fethering Observer*, called Malk Penberthy. He sadly had died, but his pupil had continued to develop a fluent understanding of newspaper research.

Given the dearth of leads in the case of Drake Purslow's death, Carole had decided the one subject on which she could search for more information was an earlier death – that of Ollie Luke.

It might be nothing. The two tragedies might have no connection at all, but it was worth trying. When Jude returned and brought her up to date with her visit to Imogen Wales, Carole wanted to have something relevant to the case that she could offer in exchange. She could get quite childlike about maintaining the balance in their relationship.

Though his fame was relatively short-lived, Ollie Luke did warrant a Wikipedia entry. The fact that he did was an indication of *House/Home*'s importance in the public perception.

From that entry, Carole got the basic information. Oliver Casson-Luke had been born in Guildford. During his teens, he had become interested in amateur dramatics and played leads in school plays. He had trained at Rose Bruford College, and his first television job, before he'd finished the course, had been as a teenage drug addict on *The Bill*. Getting the part in *House/Home* had come soon after, following 'an exhaustive audition process'. And Ollie Luke, as Spike, appeared in all subsequent episodes.

His fame from the sitcom guaranteed appearances in some one-off dramas, as well as the inevitable round of panel games, chat shows and cringeworthy appearances in unfunny sketches on 'Red Nose Day'.

Under the heading 'Death', Ollie Luke was said to have left London with some friends for a weekend on the South Coast, because his girlfriend was working down there. On the Saturday night, he had been with friends at a Brighton nightclub when his behaviour started to become strange. Taken outside to get some air, the actor started to convulse. An ambulance was called, but when the paramedics arrived, they found Luke turning cyanotic and asystolic, suffering from cardiac arrest. Medication was administered in an attempt to restart his heart. The paramedics' efforts appeared to be successful, and he was alive when he arrived at the hospital. There, he suffered more convulsions. Further attempts at resuscitation were made but were unsuccessful. He was pronounced dead within half an hour of arrival at the hospital.

At the inquest, it was stated that there were 'high concentrations of morphine and cocaine in the victim's blood'. The cause of death was recorded as 'acute multiple drug intoxication'.

When Jude got back to Woodside Cottage on the Monday afternoon, she made herself a herbal tea and sat down on her throw-draped sofa to think about the threatening message Imogen had received on her partner's behalf. She had written down the email address of its source. The platform was Hotmail, suggesting that it might have been around for a while. And the username was 'DrakeLover'. So, there was no suspicion the message Imogen Wales opened had been misdirected.

Imogen had not attempted to reply. Once she'd mentioned the email to Drake and he'd pooh-poohed it, she had lost further interest in the subject. But Jude was determined to reply, to try to engage with the person threatening a man who was now dead. The question was, though, what form of words should she put in her response?

It would be important that she acknowledged the threat. But she mustn't directly accuse the emailer of complicity in the murder. That would just frighten them off. The easiest way to break contact in an email exchange was not to reply and delete the incoming message.

Jude had looked online to see whether 'DrakeLover' had any kind of public identity. There was plenty about Drake, the Canadian rapper, and rather less about the Elizabethan world circumnavigator, Sir Francis Drake, but nothing that had any relevance to her enquiries.

After considerable thought, Jude keyed in the address and wrote the message, 'I assume you heard about Drake Purslow's death. Are you happy now?'

She sent it off before she could change her mind. Her hopes for an immediate response were disappointed. So, she spent the rest of the day worrying that she'd got the tone wrong.

The test of that, of course, would be whether her message ever prompted a reply.

* * *

At least, Wikipedia had given Carole the basics. She could get more details from the daily newspapers. In any other area of investigation, she would have started with *The Times* and moved on to *The Daily Telegraph*. Given the nature of the story, she went straight to the tabloids.

'HOUSE/HOME STAR IN DRUG TRAGEDY' was *The Sun*'s headline. The report was in that 'more in sorrow than in anger' sententiousness so beloved of showbiz journalists. Yes, it was tragic that such talent should be extinguished so early, and yet there was a warning there for all young people. A list of other showbiz drug deaths was invoked. The customary diatribe against the selfish drug dealers who 'sell misery' was trotted out. There was the much-reiterated criticism of the government for not taking more positive action. The tone of the piece was a mixture of sympathy and self-righteousness, with the latter very much the dominant ingredient.

Other tabloids that Carole accessed had more of the same. Their approach was cautious. The inquest had yet to happen, giving the definitive cause of death, but no reader could be left in doubt that drugs had been involved.

The most extensive coverage was in the *Daily Mail*. The pages they devoted to the death suggested that they had struck some financial deal to make their coverage a special feature. Certainly, none of the other papers had an interview with Ollie Luke's mother.

Mrs Luke was, predictably enough, 'devastated'. 'Without Ollie,' she was reported as saying, 'the heartbeat has gone out of our house. And I certainly never dreamed that my son had anything to do with drugs.'

There were also tributes from his *House/Home* co-stars. Or, at least, from Linda Winket and Babs Backshaw, a sign of which cast members' careers had blossomed after the end of the series. Those were evidently the two who, in the view of the *Daily Mail*, had 'big name' status.

Linda Winket (Hayley) was 'appalled that such a great talent had been lost. Ollie had so much more to give.' And Babs Backshaw (Angie) was 'shattered that I can no longer just pick up the phone to share the latest dirty joke with him. Ollie was my soulmate, and without him, my soul is diminished.'

More interestingly, from Carole's point of view, was a snippet from an interview with Ollie Luke's girlfriend, actress Rhona Revell. She said, 'I've been going out with Ollie for more than a year, and I have never seen him taking drugs. He enjoyed a glass of red wine, but nothing stronger than that. If Ollie did have drugs in his system – and there seems to be little doubt about that – then I'm sure he didn't take them voluntarily.'

Carole continued to search through the online archives. She found the report on the inquest, which stated the cause of death as detailed in Wikipedia. But she found no further reference to Rhona Revell. Or her views.

Interesting, though. At least one person had thought at the time that there was something questionable about the accepted version of Ollie Luke's death.

And Carole had that person's name.

Rhona Revell wasn't sufficiently famous to warrant a Wikipedia entry. Nor could Carole find anyone of that name on Facebook. She felt frustrated. This was her private research. She didn't want to have to turn to Jude for assistance in finding the sceptical girlfriend of Ollie Luke.

She had now got the bit between her teeth. Being 'on a case' brought with it the usual excitement. Though she still undoubtedly thought 'theatre people' were unnatural, she recognized that she might need to get closer to some of them to advance her investigation.

She looked up 'Clincham Theatre' online. It was a well-constructed website, welcoming and easy to navigate. Carole wasn't interested in the 'What's On' section, nor the artistic director's manifesto about his commitment to inclusion and diversity. Nor indeed in leaving a legacy to the theatre in her will.

'Our People' was an expression that made Carole shudder almost as much as 'community'. It implied a matiness that was anathema to her. But in pursuit of an investigation, certain bullets had to be bitten. So, on to the 'Our People' pages of the website she navigated herself.

There were endless lists of staff, with smiling photographs, suggesting what fun they would be to engage with. Carole, who had never really thought much about the logistics of theatre, was surprised how many offstage staff were required to get plays onstage.

Then she saw a much more relevant section heading – 'Volunteers'. Though volunteering did not come naturally to her, it was something she had done before. Soon after taking possession of Gulliver when she first moved to Fethering, she had joined a charity called the Canine Trust. Then she had somehow ended up on the Committee for the Preservation of Fethering's Seafront. So, she was not without a track record. She clicked on the word 'Volunteers' and assessed the options.

'Become a Clincham Theatre Buddy.' The final word prompted a deeper shudder. Never in her wildest imagination could Carole Seddon visualize herself being a 'Buddy' to anyone. She did not bother to read the duties and skillsets required for such people.

'Become one of our Front-of-House Team.' The last word had, for Carole, similar connotations to 'community', far too much proximity to other people. And the more detail she read about it, the less it appealed. Carole Seddon could not see herself as what used to be called an 'usherette', selling programmes and guiding theatregoers to their seats. When she saw that the duties also involved selling ice cream at the interval, she stopped reading. People who had had distinguished – well, fairly distinguished – careers in the Home Office just did not do that kind of thing.

'Become a Chaperone to help our talented Youth Theatre actors give of their best.' Another role Carole did not fancy at all. Though she was a mother to the rather distant Stephen, and a devoted grandmother to his daughters, Lily and Chloe, she had never felt she had any empathy with other people's children. The thought of waiting around backstage while the little egos strutted their stuff onstage held no appeal for her.

'Become an Audio Describer' and tell the visually impaired, through headphones, all the detail of what was going on onstage. That sounded very worthy, but hard work. It would take a lot of training and time watching rehearsals of the plays. Carole wanted something that would get her into Clincham Theatre as quickly as possible.

Then she saw it. 'Become an Archive Volunteer. Thanks to a generous grant from the Eric Crace Trust, Clincham Theatre is digitizing its archive, so that it's available online for writers, researchers and people who are just interested in our fascinating history. If you have basic computer skills and an interest in the past, why not volunteer to join us and become an archivist?'

Carole was glad that it said, 'join us', rather than 'join our team'.

There was an email address to send enquiries to, and also a mobile phone number. The email wasn't part of Clincham Theatre; it was for the Eric Crace Trust. Carole had never heard of it.

Carole Seddon's natural instinct was to avoid talking directly to people whenever possible. Given the option of dealing with things online or by telephone, she would always choose the former. She was afraid that if she let people into her life, they might find out something to her discredit. Though she could never define to herself what it was she feared their finding out; the inhibition was of long standing, going back at least to her teenage years. Few people, on meeting Carole Seddon, would realize that her standoffishness was born of sheer terror.

But so strong was the lure of being on an investigation that she eschewed the email option and rang the mobile number.

It went without saying that Carole did not mention any of the research she'd been doing when Jude returned from her trip to Prince of Wales Drive. They'd fixed to meet that evening in the Crown and Anchor, Fethering's only pub, which was more or less on the way back from Fethering Station.

Carole got there first. It had grown a lot colder during the day. She arrived just after the six o'clock opening time. The fire must have been lit some time before because the logs in the grate were surrounded by leaping flames.

The landlord, Ted Crisp, was standing behind the bar. Scruffy, bearded, in jeans and sweatshirt that had faded to uniform grey. 'Uniform' being the operative word. His clothes always looked the same, though in summer, the sweatshirt gave way to a T-shirt in exactly the same colour.

'Ah,' he greeted her. 'It's the Specs that Came in from the Cold.'

Carole smiled tolerantly at the reference to her rimless glasses. It never took long, in Ted's company, to realize why his earlier career, as a stand-up comedian, had been short-lived.

'On your own?' he asked, as he instinctively took out of the fridge a bottle of New Zealand Sauvignon Blanc and started to pour out a large measure.

'For the moment. Jude's joining me. She's been to London.'

'Ah. Bright lights and gigolos?'

'I would be too polite to ask.'

'Yes, I'm sure you would. Though, no doubt, knowing Jude, it's more likely to have been a conference on toe-tickling therapy.'

Carole giggled. Sharing a joke with Ted about Jude's alternative healing felt pleasantly transgressive. As he passed her New Zealand Sauvignon Blanc across to her, she had a warm feeling. And, as ever, a moment of disbelief at the recollection she and the landlord had once shared a very brief affair. It was never mentioned between them, even when, as on this occasion, there was no one else in the room. And there was the safety of a bar between them.

'Heard a good joke at lunchtime,' said Ted.

'Oh yes?' Carole didn't have high expectations.

'An old one. "What is the difference between a duck?"'

'What?' came the bewildered reply.

'"Neither,"' Ted pronounced triumphantly. '"One of its legs is both the same!"'

Before Carole could ask for an explanation – which was just as well because it was one of those jokes which defies explanation; you either find it funny or you don't – Jude appeared, hugging the arms of her knitted coat around her.

'It's colder than ever out there.'

'The usual?' asked Ted.

'Please.' The bottle of New Zealand Sauvignon Blanc reappeared from the fridge.

Both armed with drinks, they took an alcove near enough the fire to feel the benefit. A couple of other regulars came in. Carole and Ted's private moment – if that's what it had been – was over.

'So,' said Carole, once they had clinked and taken big slurps, 'what did you get from Imogen Wales?'

'Not a lot, really. She's obsessively involved in her work *as an actor*.' She put a generous helping of pretension into the last three words. 'She won't have time to think about Drake Purslow's death until she's finished her current run, *giving her Volumnia in Coriolanus* . . .'

'Ah. So, nothing helpful to our investigation?'
'Well, there were a couple of things we could follow up on.'
'Oh?'
'Imogen and Drake had an open relationship.'
'Which means . . .?'
'That they both had affairs with other people.'
'All you're saying, Jude, is that they're both actors.'

Jude was tired at the end of her day's travel and nearly snapped at Carole for her persistent stereotyping. But, as she had done many times before, she managed to restrain herself. 'All I was thinking was that if Drake had other affairs, there might be more reason for people to want to kill him.'

'Spurned lovers, you mean?'
'Something like that.'
'You may be right. What was the other thing? The other thing that we might follow up on?'
'Oh. Drake had had some threatening emails.'
'Threatening to do what?'
'To make him pay for some unspecified offence in his past.'
'Oh, now that is interesting.' Carole took a long swallow from her glass, nearly emptying it. She always came into the Crown and Anchor determined to restrict herself to one glass. But . . .

Jude had come into the Crown and Anchor with no such intention. 'Drink that up, Carole, and I'll get replacements.'

When she returned from the bar, Jude asked, 'Have you had any thoughts, Carole? You know, about what happened to Drake Purslow?'

'Good heavens, no,' said Carole. 'You're the one, Jude, who's got contacts with theatre people.'

SIX

'And you have, sort of, basic computer skills?'

It was a long time since Carole Seddon had been in any situation approaching a job interview. She had to go back to taking the Civil Service exam straight out of university. And the verbal exchanges with the appointments panel which had followed that. Then, once she'd been secure in the Home Office, there had been occasional boards when she'd applied for promotion. And since her superiors had only advised her to apply when there was a Carole Seddon-shaped hole that needed filling, those hadn't been too stressful.

'I can do all that I need to do on a computer.'

'Entering data, managing files, Excel spreadsheets, that kind of thing?'

'Yes, I have those skills.'

Myrna Crace paused for a moment and looked out of the front-room window to the windswept dunes. She lived in a huge house in the Witterings. Separated from the sea by a road and the grassy ridges of sand, it must have been the perfect place to bring up a family. Photographs on every surface showed smiling children extracting the maximum enjoyment from beach and boat. A younger Myrna and a younger, now absent, Eric seemed to be having just as much fun as their offspring.

'And what about your knowledge of the theatre?'

Carole knew the question had been bound to be asked. And all she could come up with by way of answer was an uncharacteristically uncertain 'Erm . . .'

'I see.' But whatever Myrna Crace saw didn't stop her from continuing, 'Then you probably don't know that my late husband Eric was artistic director of Clincham Theatre in the 1980s.'

To pretend she did know that would only have made her wretched situation worse, so Carole admitted that she didn't.

'Different times, then,' Myrna went on. 'The current artistic director, Lazlo, is never there. Always off doing some freelance production of his own. The staff are getting very sick of it. He's never there to make a decision, so the theatre manager, Fiona Crampton, gets lumbered with everything. Eric would never have let things get into that state. He devoted himself exclusively to Clincham Theatre, always on the premises. Oh yes, he directed, but only shows that were part of the Clincham season.

'A very successful period for the theatre, while Eric was in charge. Though not, of course, without its financial crises. Those are endemic in regional theatres. Under Eric's guidance, CT was going from strength to strength. Then, suddenly . . . pancreatic cancer. Six weeks from diagnosis to death.'

She spoke without sentimentality but with feeling. Though she had lost her husband more than twenty years before, the love remained.

'I'm very sorry to hear that.' Carole Seddon always knew the correct responses.

Myrna Crace smiled ruefully. 'Not half as sorry as I am.'

She was a large woman, who carried her weight gracefully. Leggings and boots, under a burgundy-coloured dress which someone more interested in fashion than Carole would have identified as a Merino Jersey Turtleneck. Quite how old she was was difficult to judge – she carried herself with such aplomb. Though her interrogation had seemed forceful, there was a great warmth to Myrna Crace. Carole recognized in her character an enviable mix of empathy and efficiency.

'I was talking about Eric only last week to someone he used to work with.'

'Oh yes?'

'Mind you, Eric worked with virtually everyone in the theatre. And in television – he started off directing there.'

'So . . .' Carole dared to ask, thinking that Jude would be more likely to recognize the name of a 'theatre person' than she was, 'who were you talking to?'

'Johnny Warburton.'

Carole was glad she had been paying attention when Jude had gone through the names of the *House/Home* company. 'He was directing last week's show, wasn't he?'

'That's right,' said Myrna, somewhat surprised.

'But had a stroke and was hospitalized?'

There was a silence, then Myrna nodded in appreciation. 'I'm sorry, Carole,' she said. 'I misjudged you. You gave me the initial impression that you knew nothing about Clincham Theatre, but clearly you keep your ear very close to the ground.'

Carole shrugged a 'one does one's best' shrug. 'But I didn't know,' she said, 'that Johnny and your husband used to work together in television.'

'Yes, Eric found it all rather stultifying, not a part of his career he looked back on with any fondness. Very slow medium, television, if you've tasted the constant excitement of theatre. And he found himself always surrounded by armies of people. Eric much preferred the give and take of a theatre rehearsal room.'

'I can fully understand that,' said Carole, cautiously aware of the danger of exposing her real ignorance. 'And, of course,' she dared to go on, 'it was only a few days ago that the theatre had to cope with that terrible accident to Drake Purslow.'

'Yes, it's all been very distressing.' Myrna sighed. 'Though, if there is any comfort to be drawn from the tragedy, at least it happened on the last night of the show.'

'Sorry? What do you mean?'

'The company didn't have to go back onstage this week with someone else parachuted in to play Drake's part.'

'Ah. I understand.'

Having actually got on to the subject of Drake Purslow's death, Carole didn't want to miss the opportunity for further probing, but Myrna Crace moved the conversation off in another direction. 'Eric deeply loved this theatre. In his last weeks, he was very insistent that we should set up a trust in his name to help it in any way we could. Not in helping fund the productions or in developing the buildings, but for special projects. Like this archive that we're discussing.

'It's the kind of thing that can easily be forgotten in the continuous rush of actually getting shows on. As a result, all the old programmes and things were uncatalogued in dusty cardboard boxes, stuffed away in a props store somewhere. They took quite a lot of finding.

'But I think it's important – and I'm sure Eric would have thought so, too – to get some order into that treasure trove of memories. It would be great if we could preserve costumes and props from the old shows and that kind of thing, but the theatre doesn't have the space. A written archive, though, with the material still available in printed form – and photographs, of course – but also digitized on to computers – that's doable.

'So, for the last ten months, I've been recruiting volunteers to come in one or two days a week to help with the digitization.'

'Do they do it here?'

'No. The management have found us a space to work in at the theatre. But the thing is, one of my volunteers – one of my stalwarts, actually – has had to give up. Quite suddenly, she had to go and look after her ailing mother in Beirut. So, I need to replace her, as soon as possible.'

Myrna Crace turned her eyes on her visitor. For the first time, Carole noticed how beautiful they were. A deep cobalt iris, surrounded by what looking it up to complete a *Times* crossword had told her was called a 'limbal ring', a dark edge separating blue from white.

'Were you an actress?' asked Carole suddenly, out of the blue.

'Yes, I was. That's how I started out. How I met Eric. Didn't do so much after the kids came along. Well, not much more theatre. Plenty of other stuff.'

Carole imagined a slimmed-down Myrna Crace, in her twenties or thirties, as evidenced in the family photographs. She could see how mesmerizing the woman would have been onstage. There was still a strange power about her.

Myrna regathered the reins of the conversation. 'Carole,' she said, 'in spite of what you've told me about events at CT in the last week, I don't really get the impression you know much about the theatre. I don't even know if you're at all interested in theatre. But I do get the impression that you're an efficient person, the kind who, if she takes something on, will do it to the best of her ability.

'So, I would like to ask you to help as a volunteer, working on the Clincham Theatre archive. And, if you agree, I'd like you to meet me in the theatre foyer at ten o'clock on Friday morning.'

'Hello? Is that Jude?'

'Yes, that's me.'

'It's Fiona Crampton speaking. The manager at Clincham Theatre. You remember, we met in rather unfortunate circumstances?'

'Of course I remember. Hardly likely to forget.'

'No. I was wondering whether by any chance you could come to see me at the theatre. I'd say meet somewhere else, but I'm afraid it's impossible for me to get away from the place at the moment.'

'No, I could come to Clincham. I only live in Fethering.'

'If you could, I'd be enormously grateful.'

It wasn't a problem for Jude that Wednesday. She had had a very early session with a woman who commuted daily from Fethering to a very prestigious job in the City. What she used healing services for was to bolster her self-belief. It wasn't the first time that Jude had been required to, if not cure, at least alleviate the symptoms of imposter syndrome. One Wednesday session a week and the woman could almost believe that she really was the person who so impressed others around the office with her decisiveness, flair and charisma.

The trouble, from the healer's point of view, was that the healer in question did particularly enjoy lying in bed of a morning, with a book under the duvet and a cup of tea on the bedside table. Being ready, both sartorially and mentally, for a session on her treatment table at seven o'clock was not Jude's favourite way of starting the day. But her ministrations did seem to be having an effect on the client, and that reconciled her to the inconvenience.

'When had you in mind?' she asked Fiona Crampton.

'As soon as possible, really. I have a management committee meeting this afternoon.'

The City high-flyer with imposter syndrome having been her only booked appointment of the day, Jude readily said that she could appear at the theatre 'in as long as it takes'.

'I'll reserve you a space in the stage door parking area.'

'No need,' said Jude. She had already decided that summoning Linton Braithwaite would be an unnecessary expense. And she certainly wasn't about to ask Carole for a lift. That would involve far too many explanations. 'I'll be coming by train.'

* * *

The Clincham Theatre admin block was an extension to the main building near the stage door. There was no reception area, just a long corridor, with offices on either side, most of whose doors were open. 'Looking for Fiona Crampton,' Jude called into one of them.

'Office at the end,' said a cheery girl in dungarees.

Jude tapped on the appropriate door, which Fiona herself opened.

'Jude, so good of you to come.'

'No problem.'

Fiona was not alone in the office. There was a chair in front of her desk, and two behind it. On one of the latter sat the black-clad member of the stage crew whom Nell had sent to fetch Fiona on the night of Drake Purslow's death. He appeared engrossed in something on the laptop screen in front of him.

'I don't think you know Mo?' said the theatre manager.

'I met him briefly last Saturday.'

'Ah.'

He looked up from the screen. 'Mo, this is Jude,' said Fiona.

'Hi.' The greeting carried more suspicion than welcome.

'Do sit.' Jude took the chair facing the desk. 'Can I get you a coffee?'

'That'd be nice.'

'How do you take it?'

'White, please.'

Fiona Crampton opened her office door and shouted out into the corridor, 'A white coffee, please.'

Then she took the seat next to Mo's. 'Do you do much social media, Jude?' she asked.

'Not if I can avoid it,' came the reply.

'Probably very wise.'

The expression on Mo's scarred face suggested he didn't agree with that opinion. And his manner suggested he knew more about social media than he did about social graces. 'You're missing out on hearing what's going on in the world, what's really happening out there.'

Jude chose not to comment.

'The reason I asked,' said Fiona Crampton, 'is that there have been some unfortunate comments on social media about Drake Purslow's death.'

'What kind of comments?'

'Basically,' said Mo brusquely, 'suggesting he might have been murdered.'

'Ah.'

'And I was thinking, Jude,' said the theatre manager, 'that since you were the person who found the body, maybe you saw something suspicious in Drake's dressing room . . .'

A tap on the door and the cheerful dungareed girl appeared with the white coffee. The interruption gave Jude a useful moment to consider her response to Fiona's question. She was ambivalent about how much she should say. Basically, should she mention the shoeprint she saw in Drake's blood? Fiona Crampton had effectively erased it when she put the tissues down to kneel on. Jude decided to get a clearer picture of the theatre manager's agenda before she spilled those particular beans.

'I suppose it's odd to come across a dead body in any circumstances,' she began. 'But something did make me feel suspicious when I saw Drake lying there.'

'What was it?' asked Fiona.

'It would make me sound very flaky if I said it was just a strange feeling I got.'

Mo's snort suggested that was exactly how it made her sound, but Fiona said, 'I know what you mean. I got the same when I saw him.'

Having been given such an opening, Jude asked the question that had been on her mind since that fatal evening. 'So why didn't you call the police?'

Fiona Crampton was momentarily taken aback, but she made a quick recovery. 'I hadn't seen anything at that stage that convinced me there had been foul play. Like you, it just gave me an uncomfortable feeling. And also, as manager of this theatre, I'd already got the place full of *House/Home* company members, along with their partners and other hangers-on. I had a crowd of fans outside the stage door. I knew getting Drake's body out to the ambulance would cause sufficient disruption. But that would be nothing compared to having the cops sniffing round the place.'

'And you said Drake was still alive to ensure the ambulance came as quickly as possible?'

'Yes.'

'What was the reaction when his body was taken out to the ambulance? Through all those *House/Home* fans?'

Fiona Crampton smiled with self-congratulatory satisfaction. 'I'd thought through that one. I got the ambulance to come to the scene dock at the back. It's where the lorries park up when they deliver and take away the scenery for the shows.'

'So, the body was out of the way before the company onstage were allowed to get back to their dressing rooms?'

'That was the idea, yes. And I think it worked.'

'It did,' said Mo. 'If it hadn't, there'd have been photos of the ambulance and the stretcher with the body on it all over the bloody press – and social media.'

Jude nodded thoughtfully. 'Could you show me what has actually been posted about Drake's death . . . or should we be saying "murder"?'

Wordlessly, Mo turned the laptop round, so that the screen was facing her. It wasn't open on an X page. A series of posts had been extracted from their social media platforms and listed in a Word document. A couple of printouts of the text were on the desk beside the computer.

The first one Jude read, she recognized. *'You've got away with it for a long time, Drake Purslow. But there's going to be a time – in the not-too-distant future – when your sins will catch up with you.'*

The rest were in a similar vein.

'You cannot get away with what you have done forever, Drake Purslow. You are coming close to me, Drake, and vengeance is coming close to you.'

'Be afraid, Drake Purslow. Be very afraid.'

'You will find the truth of the old saying that "revenge is a dish best served cold". Very cold in your case, Drake Purslow. But, nonetheless, deadly.'

'It's a long time after the event, Drake Purslow, but your sin will find you out.'

'So, these were posted on X, were they?' Mo nodded. Jude went on, 'That means Drake would not have seen them.'

'What do you mean?' asked Fiona.

'He didn't do any social media. Not even email.'

'How do you know that?' asked Mo suspiciously.

'I've talked to his partner, Imogen Wales.'

'*The* Imogen Wales?' Fiona sounded impressed.

'Yes.'

'Of course! I'd forgotten they were an item.'

There was more Jude could have said about the relationship, but she confined herself to, 'They kept it low key, from the publicity point of view.'

'Ah. Bugger,' said Fiona, more to herself than anyone else.

'Problem?' asked Jude.

The theatre manager's reply revealed her professional priorities. 'Just thinking . . . if I'd had my brain on, I could have schmoozed up to Drake while he was here and . . . who knows? He could have had a word with her, maybe? We'd love to get someone with the profile of Imogen Wales working at Clincham.'

'I'm afraid the moment has passed,' said Jude.

'Yes,' Fiona agreed with frustrated finality. 'Do you do social media yourself, Jude?'

'Hardly at all. I do have a Facebook page. Occasionally, new clients contact me that way.'

'"Clients"? May I ask what you do?'

'I'm a healer.'

Both reactions in the office Jude had encountered before. Many times. Fiona Crampton's informed nod suggested that she had time for alternative therapies. Mo's snort suggested he didn't.

He followed the snort by saying, rather crassly, 'Healing wouldn't have saved Drake Purslow.'

'No. Sadly.'

'Jude,' said Fiona Crampton, 'what you said about being in touch with Imogen Wales confirmed an impression I'd got about you.'

'What impression was that?'

'That you might follow up on the feeling you got about Drake Purslow's death.'

'Follow up, in what way?'

'Investigating. I meant that you might, presumably because Drake Purslow was a friend of yours, feel moved to delve into the background of his death, find out what actually happened.' She turned a steely eye on Jude. 'Am I correct in my assessment?'

Jude grinned sheepishly. 'Not far off. I do tend to worry away at things until I get to the truth.'

'Well, may I ask you – politely but firmly – in this case to curb that tendency? Cease to worry away at anything connected with Drake Purslow's death.'

'Why? Surely, if a crime has been committed on Clincham Theatre premises, then you'd want to—'

'All I want,' said the theatre manager magisterially, 'is for Clincham Theatre to be able to continue with its core business, which is putting on a varied programme of plays to entertain and educate the public.' She sounded as if she was quoting from some artistic mission statement. 'And that business could only be delayed and disrupted by a police investigation into a conjectural murder on the theatre's premises. Do I make myself clear?'

'You do,' came the agreement, spoken with apparent meekness.

'So, will you give me your word, Jude, that you will curb your curiosity about Drake Purslow's death?'

'I'm sorry, I can't do that, Fiona. I'm afraid it's in my DNA, this need to find out the truth.'

'Very well.' The theatre manager went into full headmistress mode. 'If you refuse to give me that undertaking, then I can guarantee that no employee of Clincham Theatre will answer any questions you may put to them. In fact, no employee of Clincham Theatre will agree to speak to you.'

Jude couldn't argue with that. She picked up one of the printouts of the threats and left the office.

Walking along the long corridor of the admin block, she suspected that she'd played her hand rather badly. Fiona Crampton had been determined from the start that her private investigation should be called off, but had Jude been less honest in her answers, maybe she could have evaded the total ban on theatre staff talking to her.

It certainly wasn't going to make her search for a murderer any easier.

She had just gone through the open gate to the theatre car

park when she heard running footsteps behind her. She turned to see an out-of-breath Mo approaching.

'Jude,' he said. 'In spite of what Fiona said, I'm quite happy to talk to you about the murder. If there's any information I can give you' – he produced a grubby card from an equally grubby wallet – 'here are my contacts. I knew Drake a bit. I'd like to find out the truth of what happened.'

'Mo, that's very kind.'

'And if you're happy to share any progress you make on the case . . .'

Nice to hear someone else thinking of it as 'a case'. She reached into the pocket of her thick coat and handed over a less grubby card. 'Of course. Let's keep in touch. And thank you, Mo.'

Serendipity working its magic again, thought Jude, as she made her way towards the station. She still hadn't warmed to Mo, but she recognized a useful source of inside information when she saw one.

SEVEN

It had been agreed that Carole Seddon would meet Myrna Crace in the foyer of Clincham Theatre at ten o'clock on the Friday morning. The prospective archivist, always paranoid about punctuality, had got her white Renault safely in position in the theatre car park – with the relevant payment ticket behind the windscreen – before nine thirty. Needless to say, Gulliver had already been granted a long, cold walk on Fethering Beach and was now, once again, snuffling through canine conjectures in front of the High Tor Aga.

From the theatre car park, someone more relaxed than Carole might have gone somewhere for a quick coffee, but she sat rigidly in the car. She was disproportionately nervous, as she always was, at the prospect of meeting new people. She was worried what they might think of her, making the mistake of imagining everyone else was as censorious as she was. Or imagining that anyone might care a fig about her.

She tried to distract herself by glancing, without much concentration, at the latest edition of the *Fethering Observer*, which had been delivered to High Tor that morning. Behind their frameless glasses, Carole's pale blue eyes skittered over the surface of items about shoplifting in Wick, a crash with a horsebox on the A27 near Lavant, primary school children dressing up for an author visit, and so on.

But then a headline caught her eye. 'BABS BACKSHAW ROPES IN FRIENDS FOR CHARITY TUG-OF-WAR MATCH.'

She read with interest, 'Babs Backshaw, the English Hollywood star who has been described as "well on the way to becoming a national treasure", has recently been appearing at Clincham Theatre in *House/Home*, a stage show based on the popular TV sitcom of the 1980s. "That gave me my first break into television," said bubbly Babs. "A lot of actors who're now household names started out on that show . . . Linda Winket and Todd Blacker, to name but two."

'While Babs was in Clincham, she paid a visit to St Ursula's Children's Hospice. She was so impressed by what she saw that she vowed there and then to set up a charity fundraiser for them. And she's going to do it in double-quick time. Next Sunday, at Clincham Theatre, there will be a series of events, climaxing in a Celebrity Tug-of-War, featuring Babs and her famous chums from *House/Home*. They will put on a show, "the like of which you've never seen before", to raise money for St Ursula's Children's Hospice.

'"All of my chums in the show," said Babs, "will, of course, be giving their services for free. And the management of Clincham Theatre have generously told us they won't make any charge for their facilities and staff.

'"How difficult can it be?" asked Babs. "Bob Geldof got Live Aid together at very short notice. So, this is Babs following in Bob's footsteps."

'Asked whether she's going to get an audience at such short notice, Babs said, "No worries. The moment I put the details on X and other social media platforms, the thing is guaranteed to be a sell-out!" Further details about this worthy event can be found . . .'

Interesting, thought Carole. All of the *House/Home* company back at Clincham Theatre a week after their run there finished.

She looked at her watch and reacted in fury. Having taken such care in arriving early, Carole Seddon was now in danger of being late for her ten o'clock appointment.

Myrna Crace was sitting in the café at one end of the open-plan foyer. Beside her was a small woman of mature years, who wore the expression of an overexcited hamster.

Elegantly, as she did everything, Myrna made the introductions. 'Carole . . . this is Nonie.'

'Oh, Carole, it's such a pleasure to meet you!' Nonie enthused. 'We people who love the theatre seem to be a dying breed these days.'

This greeting did little to dispel its recipient's sense of being a fraud. The response was a cautious, 'Pleasure to meet you too, Nonie.' Carole didn't want to get trapped in her lies sooner than she needed to.

'Can I get you a coffee?' Myrna offered. Carole was dying for a coffee, but she said no, she'd just had one. Her behaviour in some social settings was inexplicable, even to herself.

'Well, just quickly,' Myrna went on, 'I'll explain how the archiving system works. I'll only give you the vaguest of outlines, Carole, because Nonie knows so much more about the detail than I do, and I'm sure she can help you learn on the job.'

'I can do my best, Myrna. It's certainly true that having been brought up in Clincham and lived here all my life, I do have many memories of the theatre. So, I may be able to guide you, Carole, if any categorization issues come up.'

It hadn't taken long to get the message that Nonie was something of a talker. Carole's first knee-jerk reaction was that it could be quite difficult, sharing a workspace with someone so garrulous. But then she had a second thought – how useful such a source of Clincham Theatre history might be to someone investigating a murder on the premises.

Having made the introductions, Myrna Crace left them quite quickly. She had a committee meeting to attend. Carole got the impression she was a woman who featured on many committees in the Clincham area. And always had done.

Nonie seemed to read her thoughts. 'A remarkable woman, Myrna. Was a very good actress but gave it up to raise a family. Well, and to support Eric, of course. But women did that more back then. But she still managed – and still manages – to be involved in everything that happens around Clincham. And, of course, this whole archive set-up is her idea.'

'Yes, she told me a bit about it. Funded by some trust in her husband's name, I gather.'

'Exactly. Myrna and Eric were real Clincham Theatre royalty. Eric got an OBE, you know, "for services to the theatre". And Myrna still is Clincham Theatre royalty. You wouldn't believe it, but she's over ninety. Knows more of the theatre's history than even I do. And I pride myself on being a walking encyclopaedia on the subject.'

'You must tell me all about it,' said Carole. She didn't mention, at this early stage, that there were some bits of Clincham Theatre's history that interested her more than others.

'Well, let's get back to the coalface,' said Nonie. 'Are you sure you won't have a coffee? I'm going to take one with me.'

This time, for no very good reason, Carole reckoned she could accept. 'I'll get them,' she said.

Armed, respectively, with a cardboard-cupped cappuccino and a black Americano, Nonie led the way to their workplace.

It was a small rectangular space in a compartmented shipping container behind the admin block. The first thing that struck Carole was the cold. Minimal insulation on the metal walls did little to keep out the February chill. She was relieved that the first thing Nonie did was to switch on a small fan heater.

The workplace was very bare. A long table and a couple of chairs. No office equipment or decoration. 'The trouble is,' Nonie explained, 'this place gets used for a lot of other purposes during the week, so we have to collect our stuff from storage every time, before we can start work. We'll go and get it. There's not too much to carry.'

She led Carole back around the admin block to the stage door and called out cheerily to the stage door keeper. 'Hi, Nell. This is Carole, new volunteer joining us today.'

'Welcome to Clincham Theatre.'

Carole made appropriate greetings and thanks, much more effusively than she would have done if she hadn't been 'on a case'. She was excited by how easily she had penetrated the central workings of the theatre. Here she was, meeting Nell Griffin, who had featured so much in Jude's account of the previous Saturday night's events. Carole Seddon's part in the investigation had got off to a very good start.

'Have you come for the laptops?' asked Nell. She turned away from her counter to open a wall safe behind her.

'Got to get the boxes first,' Nonie replied. 'We'll pick up the laptops on our way out.'

'OK.'

Sure of the route she had travelled many times before, Nonie led her trainee into the body of the theatre. Stairs led up to the dressing rooms, but they stayed at ground level. Nonie punched in the code of another locked door, and Carole found herself actually on the stage of Clincham Theatre.

Though there were working lights on overhead, the main impression was of a proliferation of long black curtains, shielding pools of darkness. There were black-clad technicians on the stage, paying attention to a scaffolding pole with large lights attached, which seemed to have been lowered on cables from the impenetrable gloom above. A couple of the men looked up at the two women's approach and responded to Nonie's cheery waves. Everyone in Clincham Theatre seemed to know her.

She felt her way through some curtains to reveal another door, which opened without any code. She flicked on a light switch to reveal a small room, used perhaps for storing props or some other mysterious theatrical function. Against the back wall was a pile of dusty, sagging cardboard boxes. Dates were scrawled on their lids in fading red felt pen.

She gestured to a box marked '1981–86 SEASONS'. 'You take that one, Carole.'

Nonie herself picked up the '1986–91 SEASONS'. 'There is a kind of system behind all this, I promise you,' she said.

Carole was surprised how heavy her load was. Nonie, who appeared to be about half her size, picked up hers with no apparent effort.

They retraced their steps back to Nell's counter. Two laptops had been taken out of the safe and were waiting for them.

'Remember the usual rules, Nonie. I know you've heard this a thousand times, but Carole hasn't, and Fiona insists I say it.' She parroted the much-repeated rubric, like an air hostess doing the flight safety announcements. 'Do not leave the laptops unattended at any point. If you both leave the archiving room, for any reason, bring them back here for me to put in the safe.'

Nonie acknowledged the instruction with a mock-military salute. 'Will do, Herr Gauleiter,' she said, in not a bad German accent.

Nell grinned. 'Have fun.'

'Oh, we will,' Nonie assured her.

The fan heater had done its stuff. The shipping container was much more welcoming on their return. And the lids on their cardboard cups had kept their coffee hot.

The work was straightforward, and Carole caught on quickly

to what was required of her. There was a lot of other paperwork in the boxes, but the important data was in theatre programmes for the shows that had been performed at Clincham Theatre during the period marked on the lids. The job of the archivists was to enter into the relevant folders on their laptops the list of actors, directors, designers and all the other staff who were essential to the mounting of a production. Nonie told Carole there were plans to put the original programmes into some more permanent archive, but it would be useful for the information to be digitized, so that it could be consulted by academics or theatre historians.

With minimal guidance from Nonie, Carole soon found her way around the system of folders set up by an earlier archive volunteer (maybe the one whose mother was ailing in Beirut). And she started to key in the relevant data.

It didn't take her long to start disliking the way the earlier archive volunteer had organized her files. At the Home Office, Carole Seddon prided herself on her efficiency – and been praised for it by senior staff. And it irked her to be digitizing the Clincham Theatre programme data in a way that she didn't think demonstrated maximum efficiency.

But she curbed the instinct to say anything about making changes. She kept reminding herself that her volunteering at the theatre was simply a means to an end. She had no actual interest in things theatrical. She was there to further the investigation into Drake Purslow's death. And even though it was an intention that she would never have voiced out loud, she was there to make more progress on the investigation than Jude was making.

So, she put up with what she regarded as the former archive volunteer's inefficiency. And she also put up with the constant stream of chatter from Nonie.

The trouble was that because Nonie had seen every Clincham Theatre production for perhaps seventy years, each programme removed from its box prompted memories for her. Since, for three decades of those seventy years, she had been on the Clincham Theatre's books as a willing landlady for actors and actresses wanting accommodation during the summer season, she had a lot of personal memories to share.

Carole Seddon, who, during her later Home Office career, had

had her own office with a door that shut, was not used to working in constant chatter. But for Nonie, it seemed, every programme brought a reminiscence. And rarely were they short reminiscences.

'Oh, now, *him*. Do I remember him? Terrible one for the girls, he was. Kept bringing them back to the house. Now, I'm not a prude, but it does become an issue when you're not sure how many you'll be cooking breakfast for . . .

'And look at *her*. Went on to play the nun in that telly series. Her – a nun? Not, I would have said, natural casting. More of a character part for her, I'd say. While she was doing that show, *Mrs Warren's Profession*, she was stringing along these two boys in the company. How she managed it, I don't know, in a small place like Clincham, but I don't think either of the actors ever realized she was also having it off with the other one . . .

'And . . . *him*! He was one of the first who stayed after I moved to the bigger house. There, the paying guests had a separate entrance, so what they got up to didn't affect me so much. Mind you, I did draw the line at them having guests staying more than one night. I was charging a fair rent for one person, not for two! And it wasn't just their comings and goings that inconvenienced me. *This one* . . .' The arthritis-knobbled finger pointed at the same photograph. 'Do you know how he prepared himself for his acting? Mongolian throat singing! Oh dear, the noise, you wouldn't have believed it . . .'

Carole quickly found a hitherto unpractised skill for tuning Nonie out and getting on with her work. So, the morning passed amiably enough.

Some of Nonie's nattering had more immediate relevance than the theatrical nostalgia. Carole's ears pricked up when she heard the word 'lunch' mentioned. Nonie told her how various of the archive volunteers took different routes on that. Some brought sandwiches in from home, some went out into Clincham to buy sandwiches. One male volunteer had once gone to the nearest pub, The Feathers, for a largely liquid lunch. Nonie clearly didn't feel that had been appropriate behaviour. 'The whole place smelt of beer all afternoon.'

Or there was the Green Room Café, which was clearly Nonie's favourite choice. 'It's friendly in there, and I often get a chance to speak to some of the actors. Most of them are very unpretentious, you know. The café does a nourishing soup with crusty bread, or there are sandwiches and toasties.'

That sounded perfect to Carole. The very words 'Green Room' held the promise of lots of indiscreet gossip. And without the old programmes to prompt further memories, Nonie's mind might be brought round to the word on the street – or, rather, in the theatre – about Drake Purslow's death.

Just at the moment that both had agreed it was lunchtime, there was a peremptory rapping on their shipping container door, which was thrust open before they had given permission. To reveal Fiona Crampton who seemed to have mislaid her customary cool.

'Something's come up,' she announced. 'Something of an emergency. I'm suddenly going to need a lot of volunteers for Sunday. Could you do it, Nonie?'

'Yes, of course.' Carole got the impression that when Clincham Theatre called, any other priorities quickly vanished from Nonie's schedule.

'Brilliant,' said Fiona. 'Hours'll probably be ten to four. Something like that. And, Nonie, if you can think of any of your friends among the volunteers who might be free to help out . . .'

'I could be free to help out.' Coming from Carole Seddon, that was a very uncharacteristic statement.

'So, what's got into Fiona?' asked Nonie, as they checked their laptops in at the stage door, to be retrieved after their lunch break.

'I would just not mention the name "Babs Backshaw" to her, if I were you.' Nell spread out the Clincham edition of the same *Observer* Carole had read from that morning. 'Look,' she pointed.

It was the article Carole had read about Babs Backshaw 'roping in her chums for the tug-of-war fundraiser'. 'Yes, I saw that,' she said. 'What's the problem?'

'The problem,' said Nell, 'is that Babs Backshaw has announced that this event is going to take place here on Sunday. Not only in the paper here, but all over social media. What she omitted to do, however, was to ask permission from the management of Clincham Theatre for what she was planning.'

Nonie caught on quickly. 'Which is why,' she suggested, 'Fiona is suddenly in a tailspin trying to find volunteers to staff the event?'

'Exactly. And it couldn't be a worse weekend for her. Fiona's committed to a conference of regional theatre managers, in Ripon of all places. There's no way she can cancel that, so she's got to find someone else to take charge of Babs Backshaw's event.'

Carole thought she was getting an idea of the management structure within Clincham Theatre. 'Couldn't the artistic director do it?'

Nonie joined Nell's hollow laughter as she said, 'Lazlo? Take responsibility? I assume you're joking. No, Fee will have to delegate it to someone junior, like the box office manager.'

'Would that work?' asked Carole.

The stage door keeper screwed up her face wryly. 'Not very well. He's prone to migraines under stress.'

Suddenly, Carole saw an even simpler, logical solution to the problem. 'So, why doesn't Fiona just announce that the thing on Sunday's not going to happen, because the theatre management weren't consulted about it?'

'Because,' said the stage door keeper wryly, 'that is not how publicity works. Babs Backshaw is huge on social media. Because she's mentioned the tug-of-war online, a lot of people are going to turn up on Sunday, regardless of whether the event's on or off.

'If Fee tried to pull the plugs on the whole thing, accusations would soon be flying around that the heartless Clincham Theatre management had tried to stop Babs Backshaw's unselfish charity initiative. Clincham Theatre management doesn't care about children facing an early death. Babs Backshaw's publicity machine has left them with no other option. Fee has to grit her teeth and agree to the tug-of-war happening on Sunday, and just hope that no ardent Babs Backshaw fans get hurt in the crush.'

'That's pretty manipulative,' Carole commented.

'It wouldn't be the first time the sainted Babs has done something like that.'

'Oh?'

'She is the prime example of the star who's begun to believe her own publicity. She didn't make many friends among the staff when she was down here last week.'

Carole offered another 'Oh?' in the hope of more revelations.

'Very starry she was. And not in a good way. One of those actresses who starts a lot of sentences with "You know I'm the last person to be starry about these things, but . . ." And then proceeds to make all kinds of unjustifiable demands. She kept saying, "Of course, in Hollywood, the production company supplies me with a courtesy car for the duration of the job." She kept getting me to order her taxis she had no intention of paying for. Then she arrived late for the blocking walk-through of the show they did on the Monday. Everyone was furious.'

'Did anyone say anything to her?'

'Johnny Warburton, the director, might have done. But he was in hospital by then, after his stroke. None of the younger actors said anything. I think they were probably used to her behaviour, from way back when they were doing the original telly. And there is an unhealthy tolerance in the theatre for appalling behaviour by *stars*. The one person who wasn't afraid to bawl her out, though, was dear old Drake.'

'Drake Purslow?'

'The very same. He came from a different tradition of acting, one which involved a measure of discipline. I bet Drake had never turned up late for rehearsal in his entire career. And he'd by then spent months on tour with the spoilt showbiz brat that was Babs Backshaw. When she was late for the Monday walk-through, he really lost it with her. He—'

Nell was interrupted in mid-flow by one of the phones on her counter. She answered it and gestured to signify that the call was going to be a complicated one. The two women went through to the Green Room Café for their lunch.

There was a bubble of excitement inside Carole. She really was in the right place to find out about the tensions that had existed within the *House/Home* company.

'It'll be great,' said Nonie. 'The Green Room Café's the place to catch up with all the latest goss.'

Mind you, hell would have frozen over before anyone caught Carole Seddon using the word 'goss'.

EIGHT

The Crown and Anchor was relatively empty early that Friday evening – just a few regulars. It would fill up later. Sitting there with Jude, Carole felt conflicted. She was so pleased with the effortless way she had managed to infiltrate herself into Clincham Theatre. And she was particularly pleased that she had achieved her goal without Jude having a clue what she had been up to.

Her difficulty, though, arose from the fact that she was desperate to tell her neighbour of her triumph. For about ten minutes, the two sat in an alcove near the fire, sipping New Zealand Sauvignon Blanc and chatting idly about Fethering irrelevancies. Finally, Carole could stand the strain no longer.

'Jude, I have in fact made considerable progress on the Drake Purslow case.'

'Have you? Well, congratulations. You've been successful with your online research?'

'More "hands-on" than "online", actually,' Carole said, with a good impression of modesty.

'Oh?'

And it all came out. Searching the Clincham Theatre website, the first meeting with Myrna Crace, the introduction to Nonie and the mysteries of being an archive volunteer. As she concluded her narration, Carole couldn't keep a flush of pride from her pale cheeks.

Jude was appropriately appreciative of her efforts. 'You've way outstripped me. You've become a Clincham Theatre insider.'

'Oh, I'd hardly say that.'

'You are, though. You have ghosted your way through their defences. You – the Carole Seddon who finds theatre people "so unnatural".'

'I don't know what you're talking about.' As ever, Carole was impervious to irony.

But she did want to rub in her superior achievements. 'Have

you had any response to your email, you know, the "DrakeLover" person?'

Jude admitted that she hadn't.

'Though murder would be a funny way of expressing love.'

'I'm not so sure, Carole. Remember Oscar Wilde? "Yet each man kills the thing he loves, / By each let this be heard, / Some do it with a bitter look, / Some with a flattering word, / The coward does it with a kiss, / The brave man with a sword."'

Jude was thoughtful for a moment. The lines from 'The Ballad of Reading Gaol' had given her an idea. Carole made no comment on Oscar Wilde, but said, 'Jude, you know the old principle of detective work – well, of fictional detective work, anyway?'

'Which old principle? There are many.'

'The one that says that if there are two suspicious deaths involving some of the same people, they must be connected.'

'Ah. That one.' Jude nodded sagely. 'You are thinking that there's a link between the death by drug overdose of Ollie Luke, some thirty years ago, and that of Drake Purslow by beating over the head with a computer, last week?'

'It's possible.'

'Everything's possible, Carole,' said Jude, slightly weary. 'Were there any suspicions about Ollie Luke's death at the time?'

'Well, that's interesting.' Carole was enthused by having yet more information to give. 'Ollie Luke's girlfriend thought the accepted cause of his death must be wrong. She said he never touched drugs.'

'Often, the people closest to the addict are the last to know.' Jude spoke with the resignation of experience among her clients. 'Do you have a name for this girlfriend?'

'Rhona Revell. She was an actress.'

'Well, if she's still acting, and she hasn't changed her name, it shouldn't be too difficult to track her down.'

'That's what I thought, Jude. And I would have started searching myself, but I got caught up in the business of getting an "in" to Clincham Theatre.' Carole was sometimes like a child, desperate for approval.

'Of course you did,' said Jude soothingly. 'And to very good effect.'

Gratified, Carole mused, 'I was just thinking about another old principle of detective fiction . . .'

'Oh yes? Which one this time?'

'The way, with the regularity of clockwork, all of the principal characters who were around at the time of the murder, congregate together again, at some point later in the investigation.'

Jude grinned. 'Yes, that's something I've been aware of, too.'

'Well, it's happening this Sunday.'

'What?'

'This Sunday, at Clincham Theatre, there is going to be a charity tug-of-war.'

'I heard something about that.'

Both women looked up as a new voice from the bar intruded into their conversation. It belonged to a self-appointed 'character' and the most regular of Crown and Anchor regulars. Particularly in the summer, tourists visiting the pub took him for a salt-of-the-earth West Sussex local fisherman, with many a tale to tell (far too many, in the view of Ted Crisp and his staff). All year round, Barney wore a navy Aran sweater and a beard rather more neatly trimmed than the landlord's.

To make this impression of a 'local' convincing was quite an achievement for someone who'd only moved to Fethering a few years before, after a blameless career as a solicitor commuting daily to London from Walton-on-Thames.

'Heard about the tug-of-war?' asked Carole.

'That's right. That Babs Backshaw was talking about it lunchtime on the local TV news.'

After what she had heard from Nell the stage door keeper, Carole could now recognize another part of the campaign to blackmail Fiona Crampton into allowing the event to happen.

'Oh, she's a caution, that Babs,' a sniggering Barney went on. 'She's a comic genius. Has she ever done an interview when she hasn't mentioned farting? God, she always gets round to the subject, somehow.'

He roared with laughter. Seeing the lack of reaction from Carole and Jude, and deducing that they perhaps demanded more from someone to earn the title of 'comic genius', Barney withdrew from the conversation and reverted to boring Ted Crisp with another of his rambling anecdotes.

Carole filled her neighbour in about the way the theatre manager had been coerced by Babs Backshaw into agreeing to the charity tug-of-war.

'Very crafty,' Jude agreed.

Then she told Carole about her summons to Fiona Crampton's office. 'There's something slightly odd about Mo,' she concluded, 'but I think he could be a useful source of information from inside Clincham Theatre.' She looked up to see the smugness on her friend's face. 'Along, of course, with all the contacts you've made in the place.' She sighed. 'Anyway, if Fiona follows through with her threat to forbid any of her staff to speak to me, it looks as if you're going to have to bear the brunt of the investigation. If she were to see me there on Sunday . . .'

'No worries.' It was an atypically casual remark from Carole. 'Fiona Crampton will not be there on Sunday.'

'Oh?'

'She's going to a conference of regional theatre managers in Ripon.'

'Is she? You know everything, Carole.' Jude's brown eyes gleamed. 'Do you know, I think Clincham Theatre is going to have an extra volunteer for the charity tug-of-war.'

When she got back to High Tor, Carole went to her computer room. It was cold up there, and anyone else would have taken the laptop down to the Aga-warmed kitchen. But that wasn't Carole Seddon's way.

She started to search for any reference to Rhona Revell, but she found herself yawning. And the words on the screen were swimming a little in front of her eyes. She chided herself for having been persuaded to have a third New Zealand Sauvignon Blanc, ate a modest supper of sardines on toast and went to bed.

Next door at Woodside Cottage, Jude, who never chided herself about anything, went to the fridge and opened a new bottle of New Zealand Sauvignon Blanc. She sat, seeing pictures in the flames of her open fire, as she worked her way down the bottle. And she thought about the new approach she was going to try on the source of the DrakeLover emails.

She also got out the list of online threats to Drake Purslow which she had filched from Fiona Crampton's office. As she looked through them, she saw a meaning in one of them that she had not noticed before.

'*You cannot get away with what you have done forever, Drake Purslow. You are coming close to me, Drake, and vengeance is coming close to you.*'

The following morning, the Saturday, after Carole had taken Gulliver for a bone-chilling walk on Fethering Beach, she returned to her research. Once again, she did it in the spare room, where her immovable laptop lived. As a concession to the cold, she put on a thick jumper and, over it, a purple quilted gilet, a Christmas present from her son Stephen and her daughter-in-law Gaby.

While recognizing its heat-preserving properties, the gilet was not a garment in which Carole would allow herself to be seen outside High Tor. There were quite a lot of things in life against which she had an irrational prejudice. The *Daily Mirror*, tattoos, chihuahuas, ketchup on the table, anything on the table with the price sticker still on it, *Coronation Street*, any item of clothing with a Union Jack on it, hot drinks with straws in them, vicars with guitars . . . it was quite a list.

And gilets were in there, too. Although she desperately wanted to see her granddaughters, Lily and Chloe, Carole was on one level pleased she hadn't seen her son and his family since Christmas. There might have been awkwardness over the fact that she wasn't wearing their present.

She started by just entering the name Rhona Revell into Google. The first results that came up all had slightly different spellings of the name. There was a softball coach in Nebraska, an adult film actress from Belgium and a lot of stuff about Revell plastic model kits. None of these were what Carole was looking for.

She was faced by a dilemma she had encountered before. Social media. She knew that every single person in the world younger than her – and a good few the same age or older – spent half their life on some social media platform. She had ventured as far as joining Facebook, but she'd already checked there was no actress called Rhona Revell there.

The challenge of Twitter/X. loomed. The logical, investigative part of her demanded she should join. Call yourself an amateur sleuth and you're excluding yourself from one of the world's biggest sources of information, contacts, rumours and conjectures?

But the other, more hidebound, part of Carole Seddon still revolted against the idea. Everything she read about X made it sound like the gateway to a contemporary form of hell. A hell where scammers were out to scam you, vile trolls were out to vilify you, and crooked salesmen would blackmail you into buying bitcoins. Putting oneself on X was, to Carole's mind, the equivalent to walking down Fethering High Street naked. If she joined, she feared that her every deepest secret – even those she had spent her entire adult life concealing – would instantly go viral and, within seconds, be available for the scrutiny, condemnation and ridicule of the entire world.

Reluctantly, though she knew she was letting down the principles of an amateur sleuth, Carole once again decided not to explore X. Her obsession with secrecy about her own life – a life in which very few people had any interest – would not allow her to take the risk.

There must be another way of finding Rhona Revell. Actors, after all, don't just suddenly fall off the edge of the world.

'Oh, but they do,' said Jude, when they met at Woodside Cottage for coffee later that morning.

'Who do? What?'

'Actors. You said they don't just fall off the edge of the world. But that's exactly what they do. When the parts don't come, a huge percentage of them just give up.'

'But what do they do after they've given up?'

'Some go into other areas of theatre – directing, producing, wardrobe, you name it. Others teach drama in schools. Most do stuff that has nothing to do with showbiz . . . open antique shops, train as accountants, become gardeners, stack shelves at Sainsbury's. It's a profession with a fairly high drop-out rate.'

'I didn't know that.'

'Well, look at me, Carole. I started off as a model, then got offered theatre work. When that started to dwindle, I went into the restaurant business. Then . . . well, so it went on.'

'How did it go on?' Carole was very excited. She'd never before had such a detailed exposition of her neighbour's background.

Once she'd got all the facts about that under her belt, then she could ask Jude actually to itemize all of the lovers she'd had.

But the hope was quickly dashed. 'Oh, you know,' said Jude casually. 'Stuff. Just lots of stuff.'

Which, as far as Carole was concerned, was a very inadequate answer.

But she was prevented from probing further by Jude continuing, 'And then, with actors, names are constantly changing. Many take onstage names right from the start of their careers . . . often because the actor's union Equity won't allow two members to have the same name. Others make the change out of sheer vanity or to get them nearer the beginning of the alphabet.'

'Do they really?'

'Oh yes. So, I'm not sure where we go next with our search for Rhona Revell.'

'I'll track her down,' said Carole with the positivity that only being on an investigation could give her. 'Incidentally, Jude, when you were talking about your time working in the theatre, I wondered whether you ever—'

'Is that the time?' said her neighbour, consulting the large-faced watch tied to her wrist with a ribbon. 'I must go to the shops. I'm completely out of everything.'

Carole was once again frustrated.

Jude had, in fact, been guilty of a small fib. She wasn't about to go shopping. She was about to make another approach to DrakeLover.

Back in Woodside Cottage, she checked again with the list of threats.

'*You cannot get away with what you have done forever, Drake Purslow. You are coming close to me, Drake, and vengeance is coming close to you.*'

The important part of that – the bit she hadn't noticed before – was '*You are coming close to me*'.

Was it fanciful to think that referred to the *House/Home* tour coming to Clincham? And implied that DrakeLover lived in the area?

Then again, if Jude took the username at face value, her first email approach had been way off target. If the threats came from someone who actually *loved* Drake Purslow, then a much gentler tone was required.

Jude had sent the first one from her private email address. This time she used her work one. The reference to healing in her username might make her sound more trustworthy.

The email she sent read: 'Since we both loved Drake, shouldn't we meet to share our sadness about his passing?' She signed it 'Jude' and pressed 'send'.

She and Nonie had exchanged phone numbers, so, that Saturday afternoon, Carole put a call through.

'Hello, Nonie. Just ringing to say I'm looking forward to seeing you tomorrow.'

'Yes, I think it should be chaos, but entertaining chaos. Just hope to God the weather's OK. A tug-of-war outside the theatre is doable. A tug-of-war that has to be transferred to the foyer'll create all kinds of problems.'

'There's no rain forecast for tomorrow. It'll be cold, but not wet.' Carole's attention to weather forecasts was almost religious in its intensity.

'That's a relief.'

'Nonie, is there anything special I should know about the event?'

'Didn't you get the briefing from the box office manager?'

'Yes, I did, but it seemed a little vague.'

'Very good word for it, yes. I'm afraid "vague" is the box office manager's middle name.'

'Oh?'

'Fiona felt very uneasy putting him in charge, but there really is no one else on the admin side with sufficient seniority. Oh well, we'll just have to see how it all comes together tomorrow.'

That sounded to Carole a rather lackadaisical, even slack, approach. It wasn't how things had been done in the Home Office. For any major undertaking, she liked to have every last detail planned. But for the tug-of-war, she wasn't the one in charge, so there was very little she could do about it.

'Incidentally, Nonie,' she said, 'a friend of mine is interested in coming tomorrow. Does she have to get a ticket or something?'

'No, I gather the event is unticketed, but there'll be buckets for donations.'

'Oh, fine.'

'See you in the morning, Carole.'

'See you in the morning, Nonie.'

How long was it since Carole Seddon had said 'See you in the morning' to anyone?

About the same time that Carole was ending her call, Jude heard the ping from her laptop of an arriving email. She rushed to check it.

'Dear Jude, sharing our sadness about Drake's passing is a very nice idea. I live in Smalting and should be able to get away in the next hour or so. Could we meet in the Chintz Café on the front there. Love (I give love to anyone who loves Drake), Lizzie Grant.'

NINE

Smalting is a South Coast town to the west of Fethering. Its residents think they're a cut above the people of Fethering, but then the residents of Fethering think they're a cut above the people of Smalting. It is not an argument that holds interest for anyone not living in either town.

To get there on foot from Fethering took about an hour and a half. Though Jude might have contemplated doing that in the summer – it was a nice walk – this time she called on the services of Linton Braithwaite.

There weren't many people in the Chintz Café at four o'clock on a February afternoon, and Jude had no difficulty in identifying Lizzie Grant. No one would have cast the woman in the role of a murderer. But Jude knew, all too well, that outside of horror movies, murderers look just like everyone else.

She was a large woman, probably in her sixties, and the main impression she left was of beige. She wore a zipped-up beige padded coat with a slightly darker fur collar. Her skirt, stockings and shoes were a variation on the same collar. Even her glasses had beige rims. And it would have been hard to find a better adjective for the colour of her hair.

'Good afternoon. I'm Jude.'

'Hello. I'm Lizzie.' She indicated the steaming mug in front of her. 'We're having hot chocolate. We always have hot chocolate when we come to the Chintz Café.'

A waitress arrived. Jude ordered a cappuccino.

Jude went straight in. 'So, you loved Drake Purslow?'

'Yes,' Lizzie readily admitted. 'It's a lovely feeling, loving Drake Purslow. Well, I don't need to tell you about that, do I, Jude? Because you love him, don't you?'

Jude nodded, as if that made the lie less reprehensible than speaking it out loud.

'I loved him from the first time he set eyes on me,' said Lizzie. Jude did not compound her guilt by saying she'd done the same. Instead, she murmured, 'You must be feeling pretty bad right now.'

'Bad? Why bad?'

'I mean, now that Drake is dead.'

Lizzie Grant's manner changed suddenly. Till then, she'd been smiling, empathetic. Now, her face took on the mask of a reproving headmistress. 'Drake had to die,' she said. 'He hadn't done what he should have done. He committed sins. His death was the only possible outcome.'

There was something strange about her manner, as if she was role-playing rather than being part of the real world. But there was also something chilling about the way she followed the logic of her thinking.

Jude reckoned she needed a bit more background. 'You said you've loved Drake Purslow since the first time he set eyes on you.'

'That's right. He looked straight into my eyes, and I knew he was the love of my life.'

'When was this?'

'When *House/Home* started on the television. We had Daddy with us then. Daddy liked watching funny things on the television. He had a big laugh, Daddy, and he let me watch the programmes with him. I used to be beside him on the sofa, and he had his arm around me, and I could feel the trembling in his whole body when he laughed at something funny.'

'And it was round then,' Jude asked, 'when *House/Home* started on the television, that you first met Drake Purslow?'

'If you like.'

'So, you'd have been . . . what? Round twenty then?'

'If you like.'

That made the scene on the sofa that Lizzie'd just described rather uncomfortable.

Jude's cappuccino arrived. She took a long sip before she re-engaged with this rather baffling conversation.

'And, Lizzie, you knew Drake Purslow was going to come to Clincham as part of the *House/Home* tour?'

'Yes. Mummy found the news about it in the *Smalting Observer*.' (There were lots of local editions of the same paper, the *Fethering Observer*, the *Clincham Observer* and so on.)

'Mummy knew I was interested in Drake Purslow, but,' Lizzie said with a hint of deviousness, 'she didn't know *how* interested I was in him.'

'Going back to Drake's death . . . when did you hear about it?'

'I didn't need to hear about it. I knew.'

Jude was having difficulty making sense of the woman's utterances. Was she saying she knew because she'd been present in his dressing room when the death had happened? If killing Drake was what Lizzie's instincts had told her to do, she was certainly capable of carrying it through.

Jude began again, 'You say Drake had committed sins. What kind of sins are you talking about?'

'I used to send him letters, after we'd fallen in love, and he never answered them. That's a sin by anyone's reckoning, isn't it? Mummy says it's just basic bad manners. And bad manners is a sin, isn't it?'

'But is it a bad enough sin for a man to be killed for it?'

'That depends on how many letters he didn't answer.'

Though it was crazy, Jude was beginning to find a line through Lizzie's logic. It was childlike, but at the same time disturbing.

'If someone had killed Drake Purslow,' she asked, 'would you regard that as a sin?'

'No, it's not a sin if it needed to happen.'

'What do you mean by that?'

'I mean, it's not a sin if he deserved it.'

'Right.' Jude felt she was treading water. 'And do you reckon Drake did deserve it?'

'If someone went to the lengths of killing him,' said Lizzie with a small smile, 'then he must have deserved it.'

Jude changed tack. More assertively, she said, 'You sent threatening emails to Drake, didn't you? And posted threatening stuff online?'

Lizzie Grant nodded with satisfaction. 'Yes, I did.'

'Why?'

'Because he had to be warned. He had to know that retribution was coming to him.'

'And you would have felt justified in bringing him that retribution?'

'Oh, certainly. It wouldn't have been a sin if I'd killed him, *because it was in a good cause*. Mummy says sometimes bad things have to be done in a good cause. Mummy says Grandpa killed Germans in the war, but that's all right, because it was in a good cause. "You can't make an omelette without breaking eggs." That's what Mummy always says.'

'You mentioned Drake's sin of not answering your letters. What other sins did he commit?'

'Oh, there were so many of them.'

'Well, give me a few examples.'

'Sometimes he wouldn't look at me.'

'When? When you met?'

'Yes, of course. Sometimes, we met every week.'

'Where did you meet?'

Lizzie Grant looked at her, baffled by the dumbness of the question. 'On the television, of course,' she replied. 'That's how we first met. On the very first episode of *House/Home*. He was looking straight at me and, as I said, that was when we fell in love.'

Up until that moment, Jude had been thinking it distantly possible that Lizzie Grant had killed Drake Purslow, but not anymore. The woman was unhinged, certainly, but not in a homicidal way. She lived in a bizarre mix of childlike and adult fantasy.

Jude's main priority now was to end the conversation in a way that would not hurt Lizzie's feelings.

'Do you think you'll be happy,' she asked, 'to go on living now that Drake Purslow has . . . passed?' She didn't like using the word – 'died' was more direct and less coy – but she didn't want to upset her companion.

'Oh, I'll be happy,' Lizzie replied blithely. 'You see, Drake may have passed, but our love will live forever.'

What a very effective way you have found, thought Jude with some wistfulness, to negotiate relationships.

At that moment, the Chintz Café door burst open, loud in the quiet interior. In the doorway, wrapped up in a purple puffa-jacket, stood an elderly woman with a worried expression on her face. Jude did not need Lizzie's cry of 'Mummy!' to identify who she was.

'There you are!' she said, as she moved towards their table.

She murmured to the staff behind the counter, 'Thanks for the call.'

She sat on the edge of a seat beside them and waved away the waitress who came to take her order. 'No time,' she said. 'I've got to get her home.'

The waitress seemed to be used to such a response and retreated.

'Oh, Mummy, aren't you going to have some hot chocolate? We always have hot chocolate when we come to the Chintz Café.'

'Well, I'm not going to today.' The woman looked squarely at Jude and said, 'I'm Edie, Lizzie's mother. Who are you?'

'My name's Jude.'

'And why are you here with my daughter?'

'We arranged to meet online.'

'Oh, what, are you grooming her, then?'

Jude was amused by the accusation but didn't show it. 'No. We arranged to meet to talk about the death of an actor called Drake Purslow.'

'Oh yes, I know who you mean. Lizzie used to have quite a thing about him.'

Still has, Jude thought but didn't say. What she did say was, 'Look, I can assure you I don't mean your daughter any harm. I'm just interested in what happened to Drake.'

Edie seemed mollified. 'Yes, I'd like to know what went on there, but there's only so much time. And when you've got someone like Lizzie to look after, there's even less of it.'

She looked ruefully across at her daughter, who grinned back. She seemed accustomed to being talked about when she was in the room.

'I have to keep a watch on her all the time,' Edie went on. 'Thought she'd probably come down here. Staff are good; they ring me if she comes in on her own. Trouble is, Lizzie's always setting up meetings with people . . . online – is that what you say?' Jude nodded. 'I've no idea what she gets up to with that computer of hers. Sometimes I think I shouldn't have given it to her, but she was upset after her father died and . . . I wouldn't dare take it away from her now.'

She sighed and stood up. 'Come on, young lady. Time to be getting home.'

Lizzie also stood up. 'I need a pipi. I want a pipi. They've got very nice toilets in the Chintz Café.'

'All right. Off you go. Then we'll be on our way home.'

In some pain, Edie lowered herself back down on to the chair. 'Sorry, back problem. Whole body falling apart. Signs of age.'

'I am a healer,' Jude volunteered. 'If you had a session with me . . .'

'I'm past sessions,' said Edie. 'Anno Domini is the only thing wrong with me. That's what I've got to conquer. No, I'm not long for this life. And what happens to Lizzie when I'm gone . . .?'

It was a question she'd asked herself many times before. And one to which she had yet to find a satisfactory answer. Because, quite possibly, there wasn't one.

As Linton drove her home, Jude thought about Edie's impossible situation. When an ageing parent is the sole carer for an ageing child incapable of looking after themselves . . . It was a problem she had encountered more than once in her healing work.

Still, the afternoon had not been wasted. She was no nearer finding the murderer of Drake Purslow, but at least she had an explanation for where the online threats had come from.

And it couldn't have been a less suspicious source.

TEN

On the Sunday, because the journey was in the cause of their joint investigation, it was automatically assumed that Carole would drive them to Clincham Theatre in the Renault. The charity tug-of-war was scheduled to start at eleven, but Nonie had told Carole the call for the volunteers was ten, when they would be briefed by the front-of-house manager as to what was expected of them.

'From your extensive theatrical acquaintance,' asked Carole, 'do you know any of the other *House/Home* cast members? Apart from Drake Purslow, that is?'

'No,' said Jude.

'Pity I hadn't started my archive volunteering a week earlier,' said Carole. 'Then I would probably have met some of them in the Green Room Café.'

Her tone was rueful, but Jude could detect an element of triumphalism in it, too. Carole was pointing out that she now had a better inside track to Clincham Theatre than her neighbour.

Neither of the women knew how much internal discussion there had been among the top management about the advisability of opening the theatre for the tug-of-war event. Such a major crisis was it that even the notoriously absent artistic director, Lazlo, had been dragged from where he was directing another show as a freelance to take part in a Zoom conference on the subject.

To the considerable annoyance of the top brass, including Fiona Crampton, the meeting had agreed that the event should go ahead. Babs Backshaw's blackmail had won the day. The prospect of their being vilified online for failing to support a fundraiser for a children's hospice was potentially too destructive. Clincham Theatre spent a lot of time and money on outreach programmes, building up its caring image in the local community. All of that could be threatened by Babs posting criticisms to her millions of followers on X and other online platforms.

Whereas the publicity the theatre would receive from being seen to help the star in her Bob Geldof mission could only be good news for their profile.

Carole parked neatly in the theatre car park and got the relevant ticket at the payment machine. The volunteers had been told the event should be finished by two o'clock, but, such was her fear of transgressing any regulation, she paid for parking until four.

Even though Carole, ever anxious about time, had arrived before nine thirty, there were already a lot of people milling around outside the theatre. The doors to the foyer had not been opened yet and there was no evidence of anyone being in charge. The weather was cold, but fortunately it did not look like rain.

Carole was relieved to see Nonie was on site. She marched across to her and introduced Jude, again with a hint of pride about her familiarity with theatre people. Jude herself was relieved that Nonie showed no inhibitions about talking to her. She'd thought at the time that Fiona Crampton's intention to forbid staff to engage in conversation with her had been an empty threat, and she was pleased to be proved right.

'Jude?' Nonie, whose antennae for gossip were sharply tuned, repeated the name. 'Were you the one who found Drake Purslow's body?'

'Yes, I'm afraid I was.'

'It must have been very distressing for you.'

'Not an experience I would like to repeat.'

'No.'

This line of conversation might have continued had not a tall, balding man with something of a beer belly and a pronounced limp approached them. Over his arm, he carried a pile of T-shirts. The yellow ones had 'House' printed on them, the red ones 'Home'. Both were done in the graphic style of the sitcom's opening credits.

Having watched the stage show, Jude knew who it was. Carole, who had only seen the television recording from more than twenty years before, did not recognize him. Time had not been kind to his looks. Thirty years had transformed the teen idol who'd played Edward the Toff into something very much less magnetic. Whatever the injury was that had caused his limp hadn't helped either.

Nonie introduced him to the two women as Gerald Tarquin. He greeted them rather formally, with handshakes. Close up, Carole and Jude were aware of a sweet, smoky smell coming off his clothes. Carole assumed it was some kind of aftershave. Jude knew it was marijuana. So, he'd had a spliff to prepare himself for the stresses of the day ahead. Interesting.

When Gerald spoke, it was evident that he still had the public school accent for which he had been given the part of Edward.

He looked anxiously at his watch. 'I don't know where Babs has got to. She said she'd definitely be here for nine thirty.'

'Where's she coming from?' asked Nonie.

'London.'

'Heavy traffic, maybe?'

'Shouldn't be too bad on a Sunday morning.' Gerald looked around the crowd for the missing star. In vain. 'I wonder where she is.'

'During rehearsal,' Nonie suggested gently, 'I seem to remember Babs had a bit of a reputation for being late.'

'Maybe, but this is different,' said Gerald. 'This is her own gig. She set the whole thing up.'

'Yes,' said Nonie, with a hint of long-suffering in her voice.

Looking for something positive, Jude said, 'T-shirts look good. Are you going to distribute them to the company?'

'No,' said Gerald Tarquin, as if she'd suggested something improper. 'Babs will be working out the teams.'

For Jude, the way he spoke encapsulated his relationship with Babs Backshaw. He was her willing acolyte, obedient to her every whim. Whether he took that role for proximity to her fame or out of fear – or a bit of both – she had no means of knowing. But his need for a morning spliff to brace himself suggested fear was part of it.

Gerald Tarquin took out his mobile phone and said, as he wandered off, 'I'll try and track Babs down. I can't do everything myself.'

Nonie's habit of eating her lunch in the Green Room Café and getting to know the actors was a gift to Carole and Jude. Whereas muscling in on their own might make them look like demented fans, being introduced by Nonie gave them a kind of legitimacy.

The first company member she approached was Linda Winket. Even Carole recognized her from her post-*House/Home* career. The down-to-earth checkout girl from the original series had spun off into her own show, *Some People* . . . which then developed into a light-hearted consumer programme, *Hayley's Checking You Out*. Other sitcoms and dramas followed, but Linda Winket's earthy wit made her a natural to guest on an endless cycle of chat and panel shows. These kept her in the public eye, as did the many magazine articles about her, the movie premières and the fashion shoots.

Her online presence was carefully managed. She became an 'influencer' and, inevitably, soon had a podcast, *Linda Checks You Out*, in which she dispensed common-sense advice to allay a lot of women's anxieties.

The demands on her time as a 'personality' were such that she had almost given up acting. Instead, she was a comforting presence fronting documentaries about cruises and luxury hotels. Though extraordinarily wealthy herself, Linda Winket's common touch made her the ideal presenter to gawp at the doings of the rich and famous.

She was close to becoming a 'national treasure', though in a very different way from Babs Backshaw.

Needless to say, on that cold Sunday morning in front of Clincham Theatre, Linda Winket was already surrounded by admirers, most of whom were women. But she greeted Nonie with a warm smile, reaching out her arms for a hug. Her fans, recognizing that this was a more personal encounter, withdrew a small distance.

'Nonie, how're you doing?'

'All the better for seeing you, Linda. And may I introduce my friends?'

An involuntary pang crossed Carole's face. She reckoned *she* qualified as a 'friend', but Nonie had only met Jude a few minutes before. Ever hypersensitive to such things, Carole reckoned that was a slight.

Linda Winket welcomed them warmly. Jude quickly identified her as one of those 'WYSIWYG' actors. What you saw was what you got. In other words, she was exactly the same onstage as she was off. Jude had always warmed to actors like that. In a world where a lot of people were hiding their real selves and taking on other complicated personae, 'WYSIWYG' actors were so much more relaxed and natural.

After a few moments of pleasantry, Linda asked, 'Are you, by any chance, the "Jude" who found poor old Drake Purslow's body?'

'Yes, I'm afraid that was me.'

'I'm sorry.'

'Thank you.'

'I'm also sorry that, after all of that last-night confusion—'

'Sorry? You mean the end-of-tour drinks onstage?'

'Yes. Everyone was toing and froing all over the theatre. And then we heard the news about Drake. Most of us were going back home on the Sunday morning. So, in all the chaos, we've never had a chance to commemorate Drake . . . you know, to have some kind of ceremony, some official way of saying how much he meant to all of us. He was a lovely man.'

'Yes, I found that when I worked with him.'

'Oh, are you in the business?'

'Was. Very definitely "was". Aeons ago.'

'Right. I got to respect Drake a lot,' said Linda, 'during this tour. He really didn't want to do it.'

'I rather gathered that.'

'No, he had firmly moved away from comedy in recent years. Into much more serious theatre. Which trend had only been intensified when he got together with Imogen Wales.'

'Yes. I talked to her recently.'

'You know her?'

'From way back. Again, we worked together years ago. But I got the impression Imogen thought Drake doing the *House/Home* tour was very definitely letting the side down.'

'It was agony for him,' said Linda. 'Never mind "letting the side down"; he only agreed to do it because he didn't want to let the rest of us down. Some of the company really needed the work, and without ever mentioning it, he understood that. Drake didn't want to be the one who stopped the whole tour from happening. He was a lovely man,' she repeated. 'I wish we could do something in his memory.'

Carole, who thought this 'luvvie' duologue had been going

on far too long, was about to say something, but she was interrupted by another voice, saying, 'Oh, but, Linda, we *are* going to do something in his memory.'

Carole turned to check out the newcomer. Though Jude, having seen the stage play, knew who it was, Carole would never have recognized Anita Harcourt, who she'd seen playing Belle in the television recording.

It was not that she had ceased to be beautiful. It was just that there was a lot more of her to be beautiful. From the sylph-like poster in every schoolboy's bedroom, Anita Harcourt had burgeoned into an Earth Goddess of ample, forgiving curves. She was dressed in floaty things, lots of scarves and jangly ethnic jewellery. In fact, Carole observed with disapproval, her dress sense was extremely similar to Jude's.

Anita Harcourt was towing behind her a platform trolley, on which could be seen something large made of canvas and a set of decorated drums. Carole steeled herself against the imminent onset of flakiness.

Linda and Anita at once had their arms around each other in a hug of genuine warmth rather than stagey flamboyance.

'Lovely to see you, Anita,' said Linda. 'What do you mean about doing something in Drake's memory?'

'I'm on the case.' The Earth Goddess gestured to her trolley. 'I'll put up my teepee, and after the tug-of-war, we'll settle Drake's spirit.'

'With the help of the drums?' asked Linda.

'Of course, with the help of the drums. Can't do it without the drums. And the singing bowls, too. The spirits must be summoned.'

Jude avoided looking at Carole. She knew her neighbour's horror of anything 'alternative'. She'd heard enough scepticism about her own work as a healer. And she could almost set a watch on the time when the expression 'mumbo-jumbo' would be first spoken in such conversations. Though she herself warmed to the way Anita spoke, and though she undoubtedly took her rituals seriously, Jude could still recognize that they might cause amusement.

'Is there anything I can do to help?' asked Linda.

'Well, I could use a hand putting the teepee up.'

Linda Winket instantly called out to the crowd, 'Hey, you lot, come and help me and Anita put up her teepee!'

They were immediately surrounded by *House/Home* fans desperate actually to participate in some activity with their idols, which they could take photographs of and report to their friends on social media.

There continued to be evidence of how fruitfully Nonie had put in her time in the Green Room Café. Most of the *House/Home* company milling around in front of the theatre had a cheery wave for the elderly volunteer. To her surprise, Carole found herself wondering whether she would soon acquire such easy familiarity with 'theatre people'. Not, of course, she reminded herself, that it was something she ever wanted to do.

A denim-clad man ambled towards the three of them. Jude recognized him as the balding figure who'd tried to have a conversation with Fiona Crampton in the stage door area on the night of Drake Purslow's death. The writer Tony Grover.

He too homed in on Nonie as the likely source of information. 'Any idea where Fiona is?'

'She's not here today.'

'But she must be. When I saw on social media that Babs was setting up this charity thing, I thought Fiona must be attending.'

'Well, she's not. At a conference in Ripon.'

'Bugger!' he said, extremely annoyed. 'God, when am I ever going to get a straight answer out of that woman?'

And he limped off, fulminating.

Nonie provided identification, in case either Carole or Jude didn't know who he was. 'Tony Grover. The writer of both the original telly series and the stage version.'

'I didn't care for him,' said Carole.

'No. I'm afraid he was at the end of the queue when the charm was handed out. Possibly not even in the same county.'

They became aware of a slight commotion at the front of the theatre. The unmemorable box office manager could no longer follow his instinct to keep the premises locked, preferably for the whole day. Reluctantly, he had opened the doors to the foyer. He was at once surrounded by members of the public, either desperate for the loos or complaining that the theatre café didn't appear to be open. The box office manager tried to explain that it had been hard enough to get together a minimal number of volunteers, let alone any catering staff, but no one listened.

He already showed signs of nervousness. Despite the cold, there was a sheen of sweat on his forehead. He looked anxiously towards the security staff – not enough of them – stationed round the foyer to discourage members of the public from entering the auditorium or other parts of the theatre. Fiona Crampton had alerted the company that dealt with Clincham Theatre's insurance about the event, but they had been grudging about providing extra cover and unforthcoming about what might happen in the event of a major disaster.

Because this was the first time that day the box office manager had put his head outside the theatre, he hadn't briefed the volunteers who had arrived what their duties were. When Nonie, Carole and Jude approached him to ask for that information, he ran off like a frightened rabbit towards the admin block.

As eleven o'clock drew near, Gerald Tarquin's anxiety was becoming infectious. The considerable crowd, summoned by Babs Backshaw's online urgings, started wondering about the whereabouts of their idol. Was the whole event going to be a washout? Since the box office manager had not re-emerged from the theatre interior, it was to the volunteers that they expressed their gripes. Though still unbriefed on their duties, Nonie, Carole and Jude were soon fully occupied dealing with the restive public and making excuses for Babs Backshaw. Jude was thinking that, over the years, a lot of people must have spent time making excuses for Babs Backshaw.

The only signs of any event about to happen at Clincham Theatre were an unattended microphone and PA system, Anita's teepee erected on the edge of the park and the actual tug-of-war rope. This had been brought out from somewhere backstage by Mo and another stagehand and laid out in front of the theatre. It had faded red flags fixed at its middle point and a metre either side of that. Its surface was furry with age and use. Carole wondered whether it had been rolled out for many a fundraising fête over the years. Or perhaps it was a discarded prop from some forgotten play in which a tug-of-war featured.

The rope's presence, laid out in front of the theatre's doors, offered a challenge to the children who'd been dragged along by their parents to the non-event. They'd been standing around in the cold and were now getting distinctly bored. Soon they were picking up the rope ends and staging their own contests. There weren't enough volunteers to stop them, but then again, how much harm could they do? The answer was a few scraped knees from kids who slipped on the stone surface. Some inevitable wailing ensued.

The chimes from a nearby church clock striking eleven told everyone that Babs Backshaw was now officially late. Men with cameras from the Clincham newspapers and a small camera crew from the local television station, who had recently arrived, looked distinctly unamused.

Just as the more disgruntled attendees started checking their watches, with that sense of timing that initially irritated and ultimately charmed her fans, a hire car, with Babs Backshaw waving from the wound-down back window, screeched to a halt outside the theatre. The crowd erupted into 'all is forgiven' cheers.

Babs bundled herself out of the car, anticipating the driver's attempt to open her door. He clearly demanded payment for his services, but the star blithely pointed him in the direction of Nell the stage door keeper, as she hastened towards the microphone.

Babs Backshaw's dress sense had always been bizarre. It went against her instincts to follow the conventional rationale of what went with what. She was never going to be a fashion icon, and the more her fame increased, the more she cultivated her sartorial eccentricities. Some of the less charitable in the profession, stealing the line from the original sitcom, still referred to her as 'the unmade bed'. But, of course, she gloried in such insults – yet another demonstration of her unquenchable fame. Her image was fed by continual reinvention.

For her hastily mounted tug-of-war in aid of St Ursula's Children's Hospice, Babs had selected a red basque which made her look like an overfilled ice cream cone, a denim jacket on the back of which the word 'fart' was picked out in rhinestones, a purple chiffon tutu, electric-blue fishnet stockings and silver-painted gumboots. On top of her tangled blue hair was perched a wide-brimmed pink Zorro hat. The cameras from the local newspapers were already clicking.

There was much whooping and cheering as Babs Backshaw grasped the microphone. Her first words – 'You shouldn't have . . .' – were greeted with an eruption of laughter and applause.

Carole looked at her neighbour with a 'What's all that about?' expression. Jude, who'd done a bit of research on Babs Backshaw, replied, 'It's a catchphrase from her Netflix comedy series.'

Carole made a typical Carole face as the star went on, 'But, in fact, you have, and I can't thank you enough for turning out on this cold morning. Let me tell you, for someone who now spends most of her life in LA, this feels *really* cold. In fact, it's so cold that it's not only your breath that steams – your farts do too!'

She was providing the crowd with her signature subject matter, and they roared with delight.

She assumed a face of pious sincerity that seemed almost to reprimand her fans for their levity, as she resumed, 'And I'm sorry to be late, but I did want to drop into St Ursula's Children's Hospice on the way to see some of the kids. And let me tell you – they're all very excited about what we're doing today. One little boy in particular – name of Josh – he was all fixed up with wires and tubes, but he managed to give a thumbs-up to wish us luck. When I asked his nurses how he was doing' – her voice broke in a well-practised way – 'they said it was unlikely that he would last the day.'

The crowd was affected by a unison indrawn breath of sympathy, as Babs Backshaw battled bravely on. 'And that's the reason,' she continued, 'well, one of the reasons, why I want you to really give generously today. Now, there are lots of red buckets around for you to put cash in, but we don't want to disturb the neighbours, so could you make it, rather than those horribly jangly coins, the silent, sophisticated whisper of paper money going into those buckets?'

She reacted to some comments from the crowd. 'What, are you saying there aren't any red buckets? What, no buckets of any kind?'

She pointed a finger to Gerald Tarquin, who was lingering uncomfortably nearby. 'Oh, Edward,' she said reproachfully, using his name from the show. 'I asked you to do that. Get the buckets. Only a little thing.'

Carole and Jude exchanged looks. Both assumed the poor actor had never been asked.

'Oh, you blue-blooded buffoon!'

Babs's words, another catchphrase, this time from *House/Home*, elicited a further delighted response from the assembled throng. Gerald Tarquin scuttled into the theatre interior, in the forlorn hope of being able to find some buckets. Of any colour. Though he had been publicly shamed by Babs, he was grinning. Clearly, he got a charge from being vilified by her. Or maybe just a charge from being with her, however she treated him.

At the microphone, Babs asserted, 'This tug-of-war will be *fun*! In a moment, I'm going to tell you who's in which team. All the *House/Home* company – well, the ones who're here . . . I'm afraid some of them – like Todd Blacker – are too grand to do charity stuff.'

Jude felt pretty sure that was just unsupported defamation of a fellow actor.

'But those of the company who are here will be taking part in the tug-of-war – as well as a few of the great friends we've made while we were working here at Clincham Theatre.'

She gestured to the pile of yellow and red T-shirts that Gerald had brought. 'The participants – the "tuggers" – will be wearing these. And here, I'm afraid, is an example of that old saying, "If you want something done properly, do it yourself."

'Gerry – that's Gerald Tarquin – got these printed up, as you see, with "House" and "Home" on them. If he'd taken the trouble to ask me, I'd have told him what team names I had chosen.'

Fortunately, Gerald Tarquin was looking for buckets and not there to hear this latest criticism. Or perhaps that should be 'Unfortunately'. He did seem to thrive on the way she demeaned him.

'And,' Babs went on, 'I wanted to call the teams "Stage" and "Screen". On one side will be those who're best known for their theatre work – and, on the other, those of us who're recognized from that box in the corner of your sitting room – or, indeed, from the cinema.'

Jude could see what Babs was doing. To her audience, telly

and film had a lot more glamour and recognition value than stage work. She was deliberately aggrandizing herself and potentially humiliating some of her colleagues.

'Anyway,' she went on, 'everything will be sorted pretty quickly, and we'll be up and running. Remember – cheer on your chosen team! And put lots of nice quiet banknotes into those buckets . . . when said buckets appear!'

She seemed to have finished, but then she added, 'Oh, and during the tug-of-war itself, I do advise you to keep your distance from me. When my body's under stress – like it would be pulling on that rope – I do have a horrible tendency to fart!'

Babs Backshaw's audience couldn't have been happier. For them, it was like having Oscar Wilde in the room.

ELEVEN

They were all dying for coffee. And though they weren't as vocal in their complaints as some of the assembled throng, Carole and Jude also wished the café in the foyer was open. Some of the thirstier of the fans had gone off foraging in Clincham and returned triumphantly with bottles and cardboard cups.

They were considering that option when the ever-resourceful Nonie came up with a better idea. 'I'll nip into the Green Room and make us some coffees.'

'Will you be allowed in?' asked Carole.

'Of course.' A twirl of the lanyard. 'Volunteer. Now, how do you like your coffee?'

Half-hearted preparations were going around the tug-of-war rope. Willing members of the public hung about, offering help and, basically, getting in the way. The coloured T-shirts were retrieved from Gerald Tarquin and distributed among the unnaturally cheerful *House/Home* company. Needless to say, the proceedings were very much under the direction of Babs Backshaw, who kept bawling out the unfortunate Gerald for another shortcoming in his preparations. Jude noticed that he still didn't seem to feel humiliated by this constant carping. He appeared, if anything, to be enjoying it.

'I was just wondering whether either of you knew Drake Purslow?'

Neither of them had noticed the approach of Anita Harcourt. She was wearing a 'House' T-shirt.

'Yes, I knew Drake,' said Jude. 'Worked with him way back.'

The beautiful eyes were turned interrogatively on to Carole. 'No, I never met him,' she responded. 'Had never heard the name until I got the news of his death.' As she said the words, she knew how crass they sounded. Carole Seddon had always had the ability to say things that came out more insensitive than she meant them to be. The fact that she could recognize when she was doing it didn't help her feel more comfortable.

'Well, Drake was a good guy,' said Anita. 'And because all of us in the *House/Home* company went our separate ways after the last show, I thought today gave us the opportunity to remember him.'

'Remember him *how*?' asked Carole. Her natural caution about anything vaguely flaky had been increased by the sight of the teepee and drums.

'We'll remember him appropriately,' Anita replied serenely. 'It'll be a non-denominational celebration of the man we all knew, and a way of easing Drake's passage into the spirit world.'

Jude did not dare look at Carole's face, for fear of giggling. She knew exactly what she would see there anyway. Long hours spent in her neighbour's company made her able to imagine the familiar look of scepticism and even affront. And the imminence of the expression 'mumbo-jumbo'.

'I would very much like to be part of the celebration,' Jude told Anita. 'Drake was a man I was very fond of.' She also knew of old the look of conjecture that Carole would now be beaming at her, wanting to know details of the love affair she'd had with Drake Purslow. The love affair that had only happened in Carole's imagination.

'Well,' said Anita, 'join me in the teepee as soon as Babs's little extravaganza is over.'

'I notice,' said Carole, again trying out her inadequate skill of making small talk, 'that you've been put in the "Stage" team. Whereas I thought most of your work had been in television.'

Anita grinned ruefully. 'Like everything else Babs does, her selecting the teams has been very idiosyncratic.'

'So, did you do a lot of theatre?' asked Jude.

'Yes, for about ten years after *House/Home* ended. I even worked here at one stage, towards the end. I kept on desperately trying to make it in the business . . . until that wonderful moment when I realized acting was not – and probably never had been – what I wanted to do with my life.'

'And is that when you got interested in shamanism?' Carole was very happy for Jude to pursue this direction of the conversation. If she herself spoke, she knew she might be guilty of letting slip the expression 'mumbo-jumbo'.

'Well,' Anita replied, 'it took me a while to find shamanism. But it was back then that I got interested in the wider field of alternative medicine and belief systems. I gave up the theatre without a backward glance, and I just felt as if a huge weight had been lifted off my shoulders. I haven't missed it for a nanosecond.'

Carole found a question she could legitimately ask. 'So, what was it like for you coming back to do the *House/Home* stage show?'

A wry pursing of the lips. 'I wasn't over-enthused when the offer came up. But I couldn't let down the others.'

The same rationale, thought Jude, that had made Drake Purslow agree to do it.

'And once the tour got going,' Anita went on, 'well, it was kind of OK. But I'm quite relieved it's over.'

'Another "huge weight lifted off your shoulders"?' Jude suggested.

Anita Harcourt nodded, then looked around shiftily. 'But I mustn't ever let another member of the *House/Home* company hear that.'

'No worries,' said Jude. 'Your secret is safe with us.'

'Thank you.' She smiled. Though she had filled out from the slender glory of her twenties, Jude was struck again by the fact that Anita Harcourt remained a remarkably beautiful woman. 'Well, if either of you do want to come to the teepee later, you'll be very welcome.'

'I'll be there,' Jude replied instantly.

The beautiful eyes were turned questioningly towards Carole. 'Erm, well, I'll see,' came the clumsy response. 'Not quite sure what our volunteer duties will be then.'

'Well, if you can, you'll be welcome,' said Anita, and she drifted off to organize all of the *House/Home* fans who had been more than ready to help erect her teepee.

Jude looked at Carole's tight face and couldn't stop herself from giggling.

The bonhomie of the *House/Home* company spirit which the tug-of-war was meant to represent became a little fractured when Babs Backshaw was announcing the teams. For the 'Screen', she had selected herself (obviously), Linda Winket (who had too high a television profile for Babs to ignore, much as she would have liked to), and Ashley Maxted (who had taken on the role of Mr Whiffen's wife Madeleine for the tour and had been a minor name in a couple of soaps). When announcing this last name, Babs did not endear herself to the actress by calling her 'Maxton', rather than 'Maxted'.

She also enlisted the stagehand Mo, 'because he told me he worked in television for a while', but more probably because his physical strength could only help the 'Screen' team to win. Babs Backshaw was nothing if not competitive.

The slight disruption occurred when she announced that Tony Grover would also be on her side.

'No, I should be on the "Stage" team,' he objected with his customary lack of grace. 'I've put television behind me.'

'Isn't it more true,' said Babs waspishly, 'that television has put *you* behind *it*?'

'No, it was my choice,' the writer asserted forcibly. 'And my future is going to be in the theatre. Once the *House/Home* show is in the West End, my profile will be sky-high and I'll—'

'That's in the future, Tony,' snapped Babs. 'Or possibly not. In today's tug-of-war competition, you are in the "Screen" team!'

'All right,' he said gracelessly, as he moved across to join his team.

Not giving him time to come back at her, she went on, 'So, that's us, the "Screen" Gods and Goddesses. Now, the "Stage" team. They are as follows: the lovely Anita Harcourt, who, when she was playing Belle, used to be very beautiful . . .'

Jude looked across at the actress in question. Her serenity was impervious to cheap shots like that.

'. . . Gerald Tarquin who, I'm sure, we all forgive for his inefficiency, which is, of course, the reason we are running a bit late . . .'

The actor glowed as if he'd just been given the most lavish of compliments. Carole looked at Jude, shocked by Babs's blatant transference of blame.

'OK,' said Gerald Tarquin, 'but I won't be much use on the team, with this bloody leg.'

'Oh, do shut up about your bloody leg, Gerry!' shouted Babs.

'You're not the first person to have come off a motorbike at high speed when pissed and high.'

'I'm just saying—'

But nobody ever heard what he was just saying, as Babs swept on, 'The lovely Will Quirke is on the "Stage" team, and I'm sure all his training as a dancer will help when it comes to the great pull . . . Do you know, this morning feels very familiar to me. I've rarely been to any social event when I haven't pulled!'

The Babs Backshaw Fan Club roared their approval at this characteristic shaft of wit.

'And, as she very much represents the Clincham Theatre, also on the "Stage" team is our much-loved stage door keeper, Nell Griffin . . .'

The recipient of the compliment looked uncomfortable. She loved the theatre but hated being in the limelight. And she couldn't help remembering that during the week's run of *House/Home*, Babs Backshaw had not addressed a single word to her that hadn't been a complaint.

'But that leaves the "Stage" line-up one short of the "Screen" team's numbers,' the star went on, 'So, we need a volunteer.'

Lots of fans rushed forward to seize this opportunity. Babs Backshaw made much drama from the selection, finally selecting the fattest of the applicants. 'Tug-of-war is one of the few sports for which being overweight is an advantage,' she cried. 'And I should know. Let's hear it for the Chubbies!' Loud cheers. 'It takes one to know one!'

The chosen Chubby beamed at the honour which had been granted him.

The teams assembled on either side of the three chalk lines that had been drawn on the paving outside the theatre. The red flag lay on top of the middle line. Fortunately, there was someone in the crowd who actually knew how a tug-of-war contest should be organized. He had been in the Navy and was not going to allow anyone present to be unaware of that fact. One of those annoying know-it-alls, but in this context, he was actually quite useful.

He established that the teams should respond to three commands from him. 'Take up the rope!', 'Take the strain!' and 'Heave!' The last was the cue to start pulling.

The teams assumed their positions with much banter for the crowd and lots of cries from Babs on the lines of 'When I take the strain, I'm really going to let one go!'

The self-appointed tug-of-war expert established that it should be a best-of-three contest. Either by serendipity or connivance, the first pull went to 'Stage' and the second to 'Screen'. During the action, the press photographers snapped away, and Babs encouraged the non-professionals to snap away with their phones. 'Make sure to post the pics on social media!' shouted their idol, ever hungry for more publicity. 'And if those pictures all happen to be of Babs Backshaw, you won't hear me objecting!'

After even more competitive banter, some of it quite insulting, everyone was ready for the third pull. The teams were evenly matched in terms of bulk, though obviously none of them had much in the way of technique. The naval man barked out, 'Take up the rope!' They did so. Then, 'Take the strain!' They did as instructed. Then, 'Heave!' and the contest really started.

The first two tugs had been jokey, with much giggling, but this time the competition was for real. Both sides wanted to win. The red flag bobbed back and forth over the chalk line, to and fro. Then, ineluctably, 'Stage' started to drag 'Screen' towards them, their footing firmer on the stone surface.

At this point, Babs Backshaw, realizing her team was about to lose, suddenly shouted out, 'Help! Someone come and help us!'

Her fans didn't need any second bidding. First, a couple of men grabbed the rope between the team players. Then more. There were probably a dozen in the final 'Screen' team line-up that pulled the 'Stage' team over the chalk line.

Impervious to cries of 'Cheat!', 'Fix!' and 'Unfair!', Babs Backshaw shouted out in triumph, 'We won!'

After the contest, there was a bit of mingling with the stars, a bit more encouragement to put silent paper money into the buckets, but it was clear Babs Backshaw now wanted to bring proceedings to a close. Sooner than some of her fellow company members, who were enjoying chatting to the public, might have wished, she was back at the microphone, making her closing remarks.

'I really do want to thank every one of you for turning up and giving so generously to the cause of St Ursula's Children's Hospice.

'I know what it is to grow up in a family that hadn't got much money' – Jude had also read about Babs's 'rags to riches' backstory, which featured in every public pronouncement she made – 'but I was fortunate not to have had to face serious childhood illness. And when I visited St Ursula's, I was subdued . . . no, more than subdued . . . I was *humbled* by the bravery I encountered there. Not just the bravery of the sick children, but also the bravery of their families. Because, you know, illness doesn't just affect the person suffering, it also casts a shadow on all of those who know them. In some ways, it can almost be more difficult for family and friends.

'I talked about bravery, and I also want to mention the bravery of the professional team at St Ursula's . . . the doctors, the nurses and all the ancillary staff, who work unbelievably hard to create an atmosphere that is so positive . . . at times even joyous.

'Obviously, there are lots of people I need to thank for helping to make this tug-of-war such a success. We don't know yet how much money we've raised, but the way the notes have been piling up in the buckets, it's all looking very promising. And those buckets are still open for donations – don't forget that! How about putting in one more silent note as you leave?

'I'd like to thank my good chums from the *House/Home* family. We had such fun doing the stage show, and all of us – even those whose showbiz careers didn't take off in a major way – just mucked in, all mates together. Without their willing cooperation and generosity with their time for today's event, I wouldn't have been able to take on the Bob Geldof role and get this fundraiser together at such amazingly short notice. Incidentally,' she repeated, 'if anyone wants to call me "Babs Geldof" in the future, that's fine by me!'

Her final words prompted more raucous approval from the Babs Backshaw Fan Club. Carole and Jude exchanged looks. They could tell that they were both thinking the same – that, through her apparent humility, Babs, by identifying with Bob Geldof, was very definitely placing herself at the centre of the day's event. She'd be comparing herself with Mother Teresa next. Or possibly Nelson Mandela.

The fulsome thanks continued. 'I mustn't forget the Clincham Theatre volunteers, who've helped to make this occasion so memorable. And, indeed, the theatre's permanent staff, who moved heaven and earth to make sure today's event could happen.

'And I'd single out the theatre manager, Fiona Crampton, who dropped everything to accommodate the St Ursula's Children's Hospice charity . . . but who sadly can't actually be with us today . . . because she has a more important engagement.'

The gratitude was deliberately barbed. It opened up the question of how important Fiona's other engagement had been. Catching the eye of Nell Griffin, who knew what had really gone on, Jude grinned ruefully. The stage door keeper looked daggers at the plump figure spouting into the microphone.

'And, to Fiona's replacement, the box office manager' – strange, or perhaps not so strange, how nobody could remember his name – 'who has taken on Fiona's burden of actually organizing today's event – a huge thank you!'

The young man, who had just emerged from his sanctuary inside the theatre, still looked extremely paranoid. At Babs's words, he managed to crack a feeble grin. He clearly could not wait for the moment when everyone connected with the charity tug-of-war was off the theatre premises. He must somehow make Fiona Crampton understand in the future that his skills, if any, lay in selling tickets, not organizing events.

'So, to conclude, my lovelies,' Babs Backshaw went on, ignoring Anita Harcourt who had come up to the mic and was trying to get her attention, 'Gerry, who, you'll remember, played Edward in *House/Home* . . . but who hasn't done a lot since . . .'

It was said in a spirit of joshing between colleagues, but Gerald Tarquin's expression showed that the remark was uncomfortably near to the truth.

'Anyway, Gerry has been taking photos during this morning's delights, and those'll be posted on my X account.' She again blanked Anita, who was committing the unforgivable sin of trying to come between the star and her public.

'So, do keep following me online, and you'll find out about a great raft of new projects I've got coming up in the next year. And I would like to say that you should have given lots of money this morning to the St Ursula's Children's Hospice appeal . . . But something within me says . . . "You shouldn't have!"'

The introduction of the catchphrase rather made a nonsense

of what she was saying, but the fans adored it. Blowing extravagant kisses in every direction and milking her applause, Babs Backshaw moved away from the microphone. Anita Harcourt's announcement that everyone would be welcome at the memorial rite for Drake Purslow in her teepee, to reconnect him with the spirit world, was lost in the tumult.

The ovation for Babs continued as she stormed up to Nell. 'Organize me a car back to London,' she snapped. 'I need to get the hell out of this place!'

TWELVE

Though Babs Backshaw had left the scene with a characteristic lack of grace, the rest of the *House/Home* company assembled around the entrance to Anita's teepee. Their number showed the affection in which the late Drake Purslow had been held. Gerald Tarquin, still a little shamefaced, was there, along with Linda Winket, Ashley Maxted and Will Quirke. Jude was surprised to see Tony Grover in attendance. His aggressive manner had not suggested he might have a sentimental side. But he and Drake had worked together over a long period, so maybe some affection had developed. Carole and Jude were once again made aware that they really knew very little about the relationships between the members of the *House/Home* company.

The presence of Mo and Nell outside the teepee showed how much Drake Purslow had endeared himself to the Clincham Theatre staff. Nonie was there, which seemed predictable, though Jude was initially surprised by the arrival of Myrna Crace. But then she rationalized it. Myrna's late husband Eric had been artistic director of Clincham Theatre for many years. It was very likely that his path had crossed with that of Drake Purslow at some time during his tenure.

As the group of mourners started to shuffle into the teepee, Jude turned to face Carole. 'So, are you coming in?'

'Well . . .'

'A lot of potential suspects gathered in one place. Someone with a strong interest in solving crimes might see it as an opportunity . . .'

Carole was torn. Though she could see the logic behind Jude's words, another plan was forming in her brain. 'I think I'll give it a miss, you know.'

Jude's grin was unsurprised. 'Shamanism has never really been your thing, has it, Carole?'

'It's not that. It's just . . . I'm as broad-minded as . . . Well, you can bring me up to speed with any interesting developments.'

'Yes, sure,' said Jude serenely. 'So, what, you'll just lurk around outside the teepee until it's over?'

'I do not lurk,' came the very Carole Seddon reply.

Once she had tied the flap closed, Anita Harcourt encouraged the mourners to squat on the rush mats – even Myrna Crace managed this difficult manoeuvre – in a circle around the edges of the teepee.

Then she spoke. 'I'm sure many different faiths – and, in some cases, no faith – are represented here today. The ceremony you are participating in has a very long history, and its origins lie in many different countries. To some of you, its details may seem strange, but what's important is the fact that we have all joined here together to pay tribute to our dear friend, Drake Purslow.'

Including, possibly, thought Jude, his murderer.

'It is Drake's spirit that we are saluting. And we are setting free his earthly spirit to join the spirits for whom life is eternal.

'Now, in other circumstances, we might gather round a fire for this ceremony, but, knowing how manic fire safety officers get about naked flames in a theatre, I am not going to attempt that.'

Jude was struck by how easy Anita Harcourt's manner was. There was no doubting her seriousness, but her acting training made her a good communicator. Her manner contained nothing threatening or, at the other extreme, laughable.

'First, we will prepare the ground, find our location in the universe.' As she spoke, Anita was taking objects out of a straw-woven Ghanaian bolga basket, which sat on the floor beside her drums and singing bowls. The items were wrapped in an embroidered cloth, which she laid out in the middle of the teepee. There were candles, articles made from feathers, a wooden rattle, a decorated dish carved out of brown stone and, a little prosaically, a box of matches.

Also on the cloth lay some small string-bound bundles of twigs, like rather shaggy cigars. Because she had done a lot of research into various forms of alternative therapies, Jude knew what they were.

Picking up one of her drums – like a tambourine without bells – and a carved stick, Anita announced, 'We must call in the four directions. Over history, shamans have called them by many names, but we'll stick to North, East, South and West.'

Death in the Dressing Room

She faced each direction in turn and beat a low tattoo, almost like a human heartbeat, for each. 'Now,' she said, 'we call the Above, Grandfather Creator, and Below, Grandmother Earth.'

Having established communication with the Above and Below, Anita put the drum down, lifted up one of the cigar-shaped bundles and lit it with a match.

'Now,' she said, 'we will cleanse the atmosphere of negativity with a smudge stick.'

Probably just as well, Jude thought, that Carole hadn't joined them.

Though Jude had assumed that Carole's decision not to attend the ceremony was down to her embedded scepticism about all kinds of 'mumbo-jumbo' – shamanism being just one in a long list – there was, in fact, another reason. Carole had seen an opportunity for a little investigation on her own behalf.

So, as soon as the flap of the teepee had been tied closed, Carole had strode calmly into Clincham Theatre, a woman on a mission.

The smell from the burning smudge stick was familiar to Jude. She had an encyclopaedic knowledge of alternative therapies, belief systems and rituals. So, she knew that the word 'smudge' was from Old English and originally meant 'to drive cattle by a smoky fire to cleanse them of unwanted parasites and insects'. But, over time, the word had taken on a more spiritual significance. Human beings require so many different forms of cleansing.

The smell of the smoke Jude recognized in the teepee came from burning Salvia apiana, or Californian white sage. But it brought other substances to mind for Gerald Tarquin. 'Ooh,' he said, 'can you get high on this?'

'You'd know if anyone did,' sniped Mo.

Jude salted away the information. It confirmed what she'd thought about Gerald having smoked dope earlier that morning. And there was now a laid-back doziness about him which suggested he'd had another spliff more recently. Maybe drugs had contributed to the decline of his career?

Anita waved the smoking smudge stick over each of the mourners in the teepee. 'Let the negativity go,' she intoned each time. 'Cleanse your mind.

'Smoke, you have to understand, is a halfway state between spirit and matter. We see it, yet we cannot truly touch it. As it rises higher, it begins to dissipate and, suddenly . . . it is no longer there.'

When she had completed the ritual, she placed the glowing stub in the stone dish. And she picked up the largest of her singing bowls. Intricately etched with an abstract Eastern design, it looked as though it had been hammered by hand.

'This,' she informed the mourners, 'is a Tibetan singing bowl, made from the seven traditional metals – gold, silver, mercury, copper, iron, tin and lead. And it is played with a puja stick.' She produced something about the size of a hairbrush. Instead of sporting bristles, its end was wrapped in soft leather. She moved it gently along the rim of the bowl and a soft tone sang in the teepee.

'With this singing, we address the spirits of time and place.' She skilfully interwove the sound of her voice with the songs of the bowl. 'We give thanks to them for granting us this time and space, and for their permission in allowing us to hold our ceremony in this time and place.'

There was a tense silence, then Anita Harcourt seemed to relax, as if the spirits had granted her the permissions she required. She put down the singing bowl and the puja stick, and picked up a spray of multicoloured feathers, attached to a stick of much-handled dark wood, from whose end a trail of leather tassels hung.

'This is the talking stick,' she said. 'Anyone who wishes to offer a prayer for our dear friend Drake Purslow may take the stick and speak. A prayer, a memory and expression of love.'

She held out the feathered totem. 'Who would like to speak? Who shall I pass the talking stick to first?'

Carole knew exactly where she was going. Though staff had been stationed round the foyer to stop Babs Backshaw fans from going any further into the building, her volunteer badge on its lanyard gave her unimpeded access.

She knew Nell wasn't on duty at the stage door, but she didn't feel she needed to access the laptops anyway. Like all proper academics, she would return to the original source material.

After a bit of fumbling among the long black curtains, Carole found the props store where the old Clincham Theatre programmes were stored. She switched on the light and started her search.

The dates she was looking for were a few years after the ending of the final *House/Home* series. In fact, she could be more specific than that. Her research into Ollie Luke had given her the exact date of his demise from a drug overdose. He was said to have left London for the weekend, because his girlfriend was working somewhere on the South Coast.

Of course, it could have been Brighton. That was the location for the club in which Ollie Luke spent his last evening, a club that Carole's research had identified as 'The Gryphon', now no longer in business. But Clincham wasn't that far away from Brighton. It was another theatre where Ollie Luke's girlfriend could have been working. Mentally, Carole crossed her fingers as she shuffled through the old programmes.

Myrna Crace was the first to take up the offer of the talking stick. That was appropriate, really. As Clincham Theatre royalty, she took precedence at any occasion on the premises. She had been gracious on many public occasions, and the fact that she was sitting in considerable discomfort on the mat flooring of a teepee on the edge of the park did nothing to detract from her customary dignity.

'I would just like to say that Drake Purslow was someone my late husband Eric and I always admired both as an actor and as a human being. The world is impoverished by his passing.'

As ever in Myrna's life, the right words for the right occasion. Jude had confirmation of her suspicion that Drake must have known the Craces.

Myrna handed the talking stick back to Anita. There was a silence, reminiscent of school assemblies when the head teacher asks who has a question for the visiting speaker. Then Nell raised her hand, and the talking stick was passed to her.

'I just want to say that Drake was a lovely guy. Some actors, particularly in touring shows, treat the permanent staff at the theatres they're working in as just pieces of furniture.'

Jude wondered which actors she might be referring to. She would have put money on Babs Backshaw being one of them.

'While others always have time for a chat. Drake was one of

the second lot, always interested in what was happening in my life, never saying anything about himself. A real gent. I'm only sorry that, though I kept telling him that putting that heavy old computer up on the shelf in his dressing room was potentially dangerous . . . well, we know what happened, don't we?'

Nell let out a slight sniffle as she handed the talking stick back to Anita. That started Linda Winket crying. She reached out for the talking stick and just managed the words, 'Drake was just a lovely guy,' before handing it back.

The next hand up was Gerald Tarquin's. The glaze in his eyes supported Jude's view that he might have smoked more dope recently. And the slur in his voice confirmed it.

'Yeah, Drake Purslow was a great guy, like you say. But he could be a bit, like, old-fashioned.' Jude was getting the impression that the drug had over-relaxed him. Surely, even at shamanic memorials, it wasn't done to criticize the deceased.

'And he also wasn't supportive of the show. He kept implying that *House/Home* was crap, and there was no way he'd stay with it if it transferred to the West End. So he was, like, ruining a big career opportunity for the rest of us. And other actors, like Babs, were prepared to stay with the show, and she's got many more . . . more lucrative, offers than the rest of us. And Drake was very rude, really offensive to Babs on more than one occasion.

'So, obviously, no one wants anyone to die – that's a real bummer – but it wasn't completely bad news that Drake Purslow was killed.'

The communal intake of breath showed that the assembled mourners realized what he'd said before Gerald himself had.

When he did twig, he mumbled out, 'That is to say . . . I didn't mean "killed". I meant . . . it was the falling computer that killed him. I'm sorry he died.'

Jude thought it had probably been the marijuana talking, but she caught a meaningful look from Mo, who gestured that they needed to have a word after the ceremony.

The show that had been on at Clincham Theatre the week of Ollie Luke's death was Wilkie Collins's *The Woman in White*. Obviously, what they had performed at Clincham Theatre wasn't the only adaptation of that classic novel. The first, in fact, had been written in 1860, the year the book finished its serial publication, and other versions, including one by Andrew Lloyd Webber, have been produced over the years. Clincham Theatre's was one of many.

No doubt reviews of the performance existed somewhere in the dusty boxes, but Carole wasn't interested in the critical reaction to the show. She was looking for names.

No one else volunteered to take the talking stick after Gerald. His druggy ramble had changed the atmosphere in the teepee.

Anita did not seem fazed by what had happened. She laid the talking stick down on the embroidered cloth, picked up the wooden rattle and shook it to the four points of the compass. Then Above and Below. 'And,' she announced, 'we are complete.

'So, now' – she picked up the largest drum and tapped out a gentle counterpoint to her words – 'we call in the ancestors, and only those who wish for their highest good to join us.'

She stopped. Complete silence reigned inside the teepee. Anita stood poised, as if waiting for something.

The silence extended. Then, almost directly overhead, there was the sound of a thunderclap. A frisson spread through the mourners. Jude, deeply aware of the workings of synchronicity, was unsurprised but impressed.

Anita Harcourt smiled, a huge beam of joy and peace. Her whole body relaxed as she said, 'The spirits call in the spirit of Drake Purslow as one of their own.'

Then, to everyone's surprise – even Jude's – Anita howled like a wolf.

The *Woman in White* programme provided the answer to Carole's quest. Marian Halcombe, the less attractive of the two main female characters, had been played by Rhona Revell.

Carole was ecstatic. That was the name she had been looking for.

But, to her considerable gratification, the programme also contained two other familiar names that she hadn't been expecting.

THIRTEEN

The bowls sang their eerie chant as Anita massaged their rims with the leather puja stick. She intoned the final farewell to Drake Purslow. 'We honour you for all that you are, all that you have been and all that you will be.'

One final touch on the largest singing bowl and a long, low note reverberated around the teepee until, like the smoke from the smudge sticks, it dissipated into nothingness.

Another long silence, then Anita stepped across to untie the flap of the door.

'Thank you for being with me to honour our friend and fellow spirit, Drake. As you leave the teepee, those of you who wish to may join me outside in a circle dance.'

Most of the mourners were happy to do that. The majority of actors, genetically flamboyant, love any form of dancing. They readily joined hands. Gerald Tarquin, hazy and grinning, allowed himself to be led into the chain. Mo said to Jude, 'Got to go now – meeting about tomorrow's get-in for the new show. But I'll call you.'

'Fine,' she said, as she took someone's hand. Anita closed the circle and started a clockwise movement to some abstract rhythm they all quickly caught on to.

Though the timing of the thunderclap may have seemed magical, it had been followed by what thunderclaps usually presage. Fat drops of rain were spattering on to the paved surface in front of Clincham Theatre. As the dancers whirled in celebration, they got very wet. Water made its way through winter layers of clothing, and hair flattened damply against skulls.

Carole's research had taken her longer than expected, and when she got back to the teepee, hurrying through the rain, the circle dance was over. Probably just as well. Seeing Jude engaging in such an activity would, in time, have prompted knee-jerk reactions featuring the expression 'mumbo-jumbo'. It was also probably just as well that Anita had packed all her shamanic props, except for the drums and singing bowls, into her bolga basket. That saved a few more iterations of 'mumbo-jumbo' when the functions of a 'smudge stick' and a 'talking stick' were described.

Carole was deeply affronted by the rain. The weather forecast had said distinctly that there wouldn't be any rain. She felt betrayed by one of the authorities she had always believed in. And if Jude had told her that the rain had been triggered by powers from the spirit world . . . It was probably just as well that that conversation never happened.

The teepee flap was open. Carole entered to find only Anita and Jude inside. They were facing each other, in postures that could only be described as 'squatting on their haunches'.

This was not a bodily position that Carole Seddon favoured. Nor indeed was 'haunch' a word that she favoured. There was something too earthy about it. Animals had haunches – a 'haunch of venison' was a perfectly acceptable phrase – but nice middle-class ladies from Fethering didn't. Well, maybe Jude did, Carole conceded to herself, but Jude was never really a proper Fethering person. And the day Carole Seddon was caught squatting on her haunches was the day civilization officially came to an end.

Her respect for civilization meant, however, that she did have the right polite and solicitous question to ask in any social situation. A shamanic memorial service was a first for her, so she fell back on an old favourite, suitable for any occasion: 'I hope everything went well.'

'Very well,' said Jude.

'His spirit is with the spirits,' said Anita.

'Oh,' said Carole. 'Good.' And she thought that, hopefully, would finish with the topic of shamanic memorial services. She was, after all, bursting with her news.

'I've just been doing some rather interesting research,' she began diffidently.

'Oh?' Jude was instantly alert.

Carole still held the programme in her hand. She had had a momentary qualm about taking it from its cardboard box but justified the action on the grounds that it was part of an investigation. Any behaviour could be rationalized when Carole Seddon was 'on a case'. And she would return the programme to the archive as soon as it had served its purpose.

She felt rather awkward, towering over the other two in the teepee. Though there was no way she would ever be seen squatting on her haunches, she did manage, in a slightly ungainly fashion, to descend into a sitting position on the matting to begin her narrative.

'I've been researching the death of Ollie Luke.'

'Ah.' The sparkle in Anita's beautiful eyes showed that she was now fully engaged, too. 'You think there was something odd about it?' she asked eagerly.

'Why? Do you?'

'It always seemed peculiar. I mean, over the *House/Home* years, I spent a lot of time with Ollie. And he enjoyed a drink, certainly, but I never knew him to have anything to do with drugs. Indeed, he was quite vehemently anti. Prepared to say in public how much more strongly he thought the government should clamp down on dealers.

'Which, of course, gave the tabloids a field day when the circumstances of his death came out. They always love to be self-righteous about hypocrisy. And they'd suddenly been gifted with exactly what they were after. A high-profile actor, who had risen above the parapet to condemn drugs, was discovered to have died of an overdose . . . They could really go to town on it.'

'What was he like?' asked Jude, though she knew Carole would think the question irrelevant. 'Ollie Luke? He always came across in the series as a cheery soul.'

'Yes.' Anita grimaced. 'He was a good actor, which helped, particularly after the cock-up on the pilot. Nice guy to have around, too.'

'But?' Jude prompted, responding to the edge of uncertainty in the shaman's tone.

'But . . . he was also quite guarded. Didn't like people getting too close to him. I think he was pretty insecure, couldn't really believe what had happened to him.'

'What *had* happened to him?' asked Carole bluntly.

'Well, Ollie was straight out of drama school . . . Actually, I'm not sure that he had finished drama school when he auditioned for the part. And it all happened very quickly, because they had to recast after the pilot—'

'Sorry . . . just a minute,' Jude interrupted. 'You mentioned a "cock-up" on the pilot earlier. I haven't heard about this. What happened?'

'Oh, I thought everyone knew, but of course you wouldn't.'

Anita Harcourt seemed quite happy to continue squatting on her haunches as she launched into her explanation. Carole assumed that learning to do that was one of the first subjects you dealt with in shaman training (Week One, Day One – Elementary Haunch-Squatting). But she was pleased to see that Jude had slumped back into a sitting position like hers.

'OK,' Anita began, 'as you may know, *House/Home* was written by someone called Tony Grover.'

'Yes, we've met him,' said Jude.

'Not a very prepossessing character,' Carole observed.

'No, maybe not,' Anita agreed. She wasn't the sort of performer who would ever badmouth people she had worked with.

'We saw him earlier,' said Jude. 'Is he still around?'

'Probably in The Feathers,' Anita replied. 'Nearest pub to the theatre. Favoured by the stage crew. Tony spent most of his time in there during the Clincham run of *House/Home*.'

'He has a drink problem?' asked Carole.

'He doesn't see it that way. Everyone else does. Familiar story. Anyway, as I say, Tony wrote the scripts, and the shows were produced and directed by a guy called Johnny Warburton.'

'He's the one who had a stroke at the beginning of your Clincham run?' said Jude.

'Exactly.' Anita Harcourt glanced at her watch. Carole noticed with irritation that it had a large round face and was attached to its owner's wrist by a colourful ribbon. Just like Jude's.

'I'm hoping to get to see him this afternoon before I go back home.'

'Where is home?' asked Carole. After all, where *did* shamans live?

'Not far away,' said Anita. 'Southern edge of the South Downs. Village called Weldisham.'

'Oh, we know it,' said Carole, not mentioning that she and

Jude had solved a murder there. 'There's a pub called the Hare and Hounds.'

'That's right.'

'We live in Fethering,' said Jude.

'Oh? Almost neighbours.'

'Anyway,' asked Carole briskly, before Anita and Jude started setting up a shamanistic encounter group, 'are you saying that Johnny Warburton is still in hospital?'

'That's right. Private wing of St Clare's.' Anita screwed up her face ruefully. 'I'm not sure he'll be coming out.'

'Oh dear,' said Jude.

'Anyway,' Carole pressed on, 'you were telling us about Ollie Luke coming into the television show at short notice . . .'

'Yes. As I say, Johnny plucked him out of drama school and suddenly this kid of twenty is in a top-ten-ranking sitcom, and everyone recognizes him in the street and . . . Well, most of us in the show had already had a bit of that kind of exposure, so we knew how to deal with it, but for Ollie it was a whole new experience, and it took him a while to get used to it.'

'But he didn't turn to drugs,' asked Jude, 'to help him cope?'

'Absolutely not. Too much booze occasionally, but no worse than any other kid of that age.'

'Why,' asked Jude, 'was the part of Spike recast after the pilot?'

'Basically, because the actor playing it in the pilot couldn't act.'

'Ah,' said Jude. 'So, how did he get the part?'

'Hm.' A rueful grin from Anita. 'I'm afraid Johnny Warburton always had an eye for a pretty boy.'

'Are you saying,' asked Carole, 'that he is homosexual?'

Jude couldn't suppress a small giggle.

'I'm not sure,' said Anita, 'that many people would use that word now, but, yes, that is what I'm saying. Johnny Warburton is flamboyantly "homosexual", in a way that, in these enlightened times, one might have thought had gone out of fashion. But the theatre has always had an affection for a screaming queen. And Johnny certainly lives up to the image.'

'Ah,' said Carole. She was no more prejudiced than anyone

of her upbringing might be, but that meant she was quite prejudiced. She approved of the increasing tolerance she had witnessed during her lifetime, but middle-class values are hard to shake off completely.

'So, anyway,' Anita picked up her narrative, 'I'm afraid Johnny was more swayed by the original actor's looks than his acting talent, and the fact that the boy had none of the latter did rather show when the pilot recording was played to the broadcasting chiefs. Their diktat was that the show could go ahead, but not with that actor. Which is how Ollie Luke was cast in the series.'

'Having seen him in the show,' said Jude, 'I would say he was quite a pretty boy, too.'

'Yup. Johnny Warburton was replacing like with like. Except, of course, Ollie had bucketfuls of talent. But he and Gerald Tarquin were both very pretty, something that appealed to viewers of all persuasions.'

'But then, later, Ollie had a girlfriend,' said Carole flatly.

'I think one of the reasons he was, as I said, guarded about getting close to people was because he was very uncertain about his sexuality. He'd got Johnny coming on to him, for a start, and there was a bit of backstage gossip about how he'd got the part. Then there was the fan mail . . . mostly actual letters back then. We're talking about the 1980s, after all. No social media . . . amazing to think how relatively recently all that has crept up on us. But Ollie got loads of letters. He seems to have become, whether he liked it or not – and I'm pretty sure he didn't like it – a kind of gay icon.'

'He found it all very confusing,' she concluded.

'But the girlfriend.' Carole insisted. 'Rhona Revell. When did that happen?'

'I'm not sure when it started exactly. I rarely saw Ollie back then. You know, we were in different shows, touring stuff, abroad filming. We pretty much lost touch. But I did hear through friends in the business that he and Rhona Revell had got together. Good news, from all accounts. She seemed to have settled his identity problems for good. There was talk of them getting married, I heard.'

'But then you saw Ollie Luke here at Clincham shortly before he died,' Carole pronounced with pride.

Jude looked at her neighbour in some amazement. Where had that bombshell come from?

Anita looked less surprised. 'Yes, you're right,' she said.

Carole flourished the programme. 'Here for a production of *The Woman in White*. In which Rhona Revell, Ollie Luke's girlfriend, played Marian Halcombe.'

'Exactly.'

'And Anita Harcourt played Laura Fairlie.'

'Congratulations on your research,' said Anita with a hint of dryness.

'I assume,' Carole continued, growing more confident as her assumptions were confirmed, 'that *The Woman in White* was the production Ollie Luke came down to the South Coast to see?'

'You're right.'

'So, you were here when the news of Ollie Luke's death broke?'

Finally, Anita Harcourt raised herself elegantly from her haunches and sat on the teepee's earthen floor with the two other women. The change of posture seemed not to be prompted by stress or discomfort.

'Well, no,' she replied. 'By the time I heard about Ollie, I was back home. In London then. You see, it was on the Saturday, the last night, that Ollie had gone to Brighton. With some friends from the theatre. He'd seen the show, *The Woman in White*, on the Friday evening, stayed in a Clincham hotel on the Friday night, with Rhona. The plan was that when the show had come down on the Saturday, Rhona would get a cab to Brighton to join him at a club.'

'The Gryphon Club, that would be,' said Carole, smugly proud of her knowledge.

'Exactly,' said Anita. 'Ollie and Rhona were booked into a Brighton hotel for the next two nights.'

Carole asked, 'Did she hear the news about Ollie before she got the cab to Brighton?'

Anita shook her head. 'No, she went all the way over there. I remember, the last time I saw her that evening was when she got the cab from the stage door. She had some friends with her who'd come from London to see the show. Possibly some of the stage crew went to The Gryphon in another cab. I spent the night in my digs down here and didn't hear about Ollie's death until the radio news on the Sunday morning.'

'So,' said Jude, appalled by the idea, 'Rhona had arrived at the Brighton club to find her boyfriend dead?'

'Well, technically, she arrived to find her boyfriend had been taken to hospital. But he had died before she got there.'

That got a perfunctory 'How awful for her' from Carole, followed by the question, 'And was that the last time you saw Rhona?'

'No, no. I saw her a lot after that. She was convinced that Ollie Luke's death was caused by foul play. She was trying to get everyone she knew to back up her theory.'

'With a view to what?' asked Carole.

'With a view to getting the coroner's verdict reversed and a police murder investigation started.'

'But presumably she had no luck?' Jude suggested gently.

'No. It was one woman's voice against the entire British establishment.'

'Did you think it was murder?' Carole asked eagerly.

Anita shrugged. 'I didn't know. I hadn't been there when it happened. I had insufficient information. But Rhona was absolutely convinced of it, and I suppose I was swayed by her passion.'

'Have you seen much of her recently?' asked Carole.

'Not for a while, no. After about six months of doing what she called "getting justice for Ollie Luke", she became very disillusioned. I think she probably had some kind of breakdown. Gave up the theatre, anyway.'

Carole was once again struck, as someone who knew little of that world, how many actors seemed to give up the theatre. Or, in many cases, had the theatre give up on them. There was a kind of easy assumption that because she saw the same faces still busily employed into their eighties, that was the career pattern for all in the profession. She was quickly coming to realize that assumption was wrong.

'It was around that time,' Anita went on, 'that I had my revelation, too.'

'That you didn't want to continue in the theatre?'

'Exactly that, Jude. I realized there was more to life than learning lines, going through the mental agonies of stage fright and having short, messy relationships with other actors. I saw the light.'

'And that,' said Carole ungraciously, 'was when you started on your' – with an effort, she avoided using the words 'mumbo-jumbo' – 'exploration of alternative therapies?'

'Yes,' Anita confirmed. 'My parents were very religious. Church of England, but High Church. In my teens, I very quickly realized I didn't want to be part of that. But I did feel that in my life there was a spiritual void that needed filling.'

Jude avoided catching the censorious eye of her neighbour.

'So, I started reading about alternative belief systems. One of the advantages of acting in touring shows is that you get plenty of time to read. More useful and less harmful than the route lots of actors go down . . . drinking too much and having unsuitable affairs. And, as I read, I became more aware of the impermanence of our daily lives and the durability and continuity of the spirit world.'

Again, Jude studiously avoided eye contact with Carole, as Anita went on, 'And, increasingly, I realized how little I was being nurtured by being an actor. Somehow, the way Rhona Revell was able to give up the business, just like that – though, obviously, for very different reasons – well, it made me think I could do the same. Give up being an actor and follow the spiritual path that had been calling out to me for so long.'

Jude nodded approval and then asked, 'Do you know in which direction Rhona Revell went, after she gave up the theatre?'

'I'm afraid not. Certainly not the same way as I did. She had become obsessed about the dangers of drugs, which is hardly surprising, given what happened to Ollie. She talked about training as some kind of drug counsellor or therapist, though whether she went through with it, I have no idea.'

'Was Rhona Revell her real name?' asked Carole suddenly.

Anita chuckled. 'I never asked. Sounds a bit theatrical, doesn't it? But maybe her parents had a taste for the theatrical.'

Jude was thoughtful. 'So, what have we got in the way of information, if we try to track her down? A woman about our age . . . possibly still called Rhona Revell . . . possibly working in drug rehabilitation or something like that. Anything else, Anita?'

'Not a lot. Oh, one thing . . . Along with giving up the theatre,

Rhona said she was going to give up London. The two things were too closely associated in her mind, perhaps. But she certainly planned to live out of London.'

'No indication of where?'

'No, Carole.' A silence. 'Well, she did say she might look around here, because Clincham was the last place she'd been truly happy. That last night with Ollie . . . But maybe she was just being sentimental. I've no way of knowing whether she went through with it.'

'You don't have a phone number for her, do you, Anita?' asked Carole.

'I might do.' The shaman reached into the pocket of her jeans for a phone and started scanning it. 'But we are talking thirty years ago. It'd be a landline, and the chances she'd still be living in the same place . . .' Anita looked at her screen. 'Oh, I have found one, but, as I say, the chances Rhona is still using the same number . . .'

'It's worth trying.' Carole, on a roll of unaccustomed confidence, took down the details and immediately rang the number. She switched on the speaker so that the other two women could hear.

The phone rang and then cut to an outgoing message. 'This is Katie Clithero's phone. If you want to leave a message, please speak after the bleep.'

In precise tones, Carole announced, 'My name is Carole Seddon. If you are the actress who used to be called Rhona Revell and you wish to discuss the circumstances of Ollie Luke's death, please call me back.'

'Short and to the point,' Anita observed.

'That's the best way to be,' Carole asserted. 'No point in giving too much detail.'

'No.' Jude grinned. 'Particularly if you haven't got "too much detail" to give.'

Carole's bubble of optimism was quickly deflating. 'Now, we'll just have to see whether we get a call back.'

'If the person you've left a message for,' said Anita, 'was once called Rhona Revell, you'll *definitely* get a call back.'

She looked at her watch. 'Now, if I'm going to get to see Johnny Warburton, I must get this teepee down.'

'Can we help you?' asked Jude.

Carole wasn't very keen on the 'we'. Teepee-dismantling was rather a mundane task for someone who had just achieved a feat of research on the scale she had.

'It's all right,' said Anita. 'I'm glad to say there are still some hardcore *House/Home* fans around who would be delighted to help me with taking down my teepee. Taking photographs all the while to post online.'

Which sounded very satisfactory.

'Ooh,' said Carole, suddenly remembering another part of her programme research. 'Another person involved in the television series was also involved in the production of *The Woman in White*.'

'Who?'

'Tony Grover. He adapted the novel.'

When she left the teepee, Carole was so excited that she forgot to take the precious programme. Jude picked it up and was glancing through when she saw another name she recognized.

Mo Pascoe was listed as 'Deputy Stage Manager' for *The Woman in White*.

Which meant that he was working at Clincham Theatre that night. And was off the list of people who might have been at The Gryphon Club in Brighton, injecting Ollie Luke with a fatal overdose.

FOURTEEN

The Feathers was not one of those pubs that felt the need to be trendy. Situated near the main shopper's car park in Clincham, it hadn't considered the prospect of a makeover for over thirty years. The passing trade from Clincham Theatre, pre-show dinners for the punters and late-night drink-ins for the stage crew kept the tills ringing healthily. Saturdays and Sundays, The Feathers was open and serving food all day. The management worked on the 'if it ain't broke, don't fix it' principle, and had done so for many successful years.

Carole and Jude found Tony Grover sitting at a table on his own, facing a half-full pint of Guinness with a despondent air. For him, a despondent air seemed to be a permanent feature.

The confidence that being on a case gave Carole made her go straight up to him and say, almost brusquely, 'You're Tony Grover, aren't you? You wrote *House/Home*.'

Pleasure at being recognized mingled in his face with suspicion as to who was recognizing him. He didn't remember Carole from their brief introduction earlier in the day. But he admitted to his identity.

'Terrific show,' said Jude, who had always had more dexterity with small talk than her neighbour. 'I hope you don't mind us just cornering you like this, but we're both such big fans of the telly series.'

Carole's pale blue eyes shot a beady look at her neighbour. But she quickly understood the wisdom of Jude's words. All writers feel themselves to be starved of praise and are pathetically grateful for any form of commendation. Jude had found the most efficient way to break through any reserve Tony Grover might have had.

'Glad to hear it. You're clearly women of discrimination,' he said, a trace of truculence mingling with flirtatiousness in his voice. 'And the stage show was bloody good, too. Though you wouldn't know it from the way Clincham Theatre presented the thing.'

'Oh?' said Jude, aware that only a minimal prompt would be needed to release a flow of criticism.

'Do you know,' said Tony Grover, full of bile, 'they didn't get a single London critic down to review the production? And the publicity they set up for the show was minimal. Worse than minimal – there wasn't any.'

'Maybe,' Jude suggested emolliently, 'they reckoned such a well-loved television series didn't need any publicity.'

'That's not the point,' Tony countered. 'Show business still works a lot on word of mouth. You want your show to be the one everybody's talking about. And for people to talk about it, they have to bloody know it's on. Clincham Theatre showed no interest in promoting the stage version of *House/Home*. How many London producers did they invite down to see the show? A big round zero. If the show does transfer to the West End, it'll be in spite of the efforts of Clincham Theatre management.'

'And what are the chances of it transferring?' asked Jude tentatively.

'Don't ask me! I'm only the bloody writer. No one tells me anything about what's going on. And these things have to happen quickly. The actors signed option clauses in their tour contracts, agreeing to make themselves available in the event of a West End transfer, but there's a time limit on how long they can be held to that. So, if something doesn't happen bloody soon, the whole show's dead in the water.'

'But if it does transfer,' asked Jude, 'the whole company will want to stay with the show, won't they?' She knew part of the answer to her question, but she still wanted to hear Tony Grover's response.

'Oh yes, they're all right behind it,' he lied. 'Really enjoyed being back together for the tour. Babs Backshaw's been offered all kinds of projects to go straight into, but she'd rather do *House/Home* in the West End. Then . . . who knows? Transfer to Broadway's a possibility.

'And with that kind of exposure, there could well be a revival of interest in bringing the characters back in a new telly series. *House/Home* forty years on. I've got lots of ideas for storylines on that. No worries,' he concluded, 'all the company are very keen to go on with the show.'

'Except,' said Carole waspishly, 'for Drake Purslow.'

'Yes, sad business, that.' His minimal homage to the dead man paid, Tony went on, 'But Drake's not irreplaceable. There are plenty of actors that age with sitcom experience. Would be easy to recast.'

Carole still had her volunteer's ID on the lanyard round her neck. The writer wasn't to know how brief had been her acquaintance with Clincham Theatre. 'I heard rumours backstage,' she said, with all the assurance of someone who'd spent a lifetime in the theatrical milieu, 'that Drake Purslow didn't want to have anything more to do with the project after the end of the tour.'

The writer shrugged off the suggestion. 'Oh, actors always say that kind of thing. You know, halfway through a tour, they're a bit jaded with all the travelling and what-have-you. They say they don't want to go on with the show. But mention the idea of someone else taking the part and they're very suddenly changing their minds.'

Carole persisted, 'Did you get on all right with Drake Purslow?'

'Sure. We've known each other from way back. And he did owe me a big debt of gratitude.'

'Oh? What for?'

Tony Grover looked bewildered by Carole's lack of understanding. 'Well, obviously . . . because I had created for him one of the classic sitcom roles. Drake was never going to go anywhere without people shouting "Let's just give it a minute, shall we?" at him. And that was all down to me. Few actors achieve that kind of iconic status.'

Maybe not, thought Jude, but in Drake Purslow's case, that was exactly the kind of 'iconic status' that he didn't want. And Imogen Wales certainly didn't want a sitcom catchphrase associated with anyone she spent time with. It did not fit in with the kind of classical theatre she and the mature Drake Purslow aspired to.

Jude moved on to a more direct question. 'Did it ever occur to you that there might be something odd about Drake Purslow's death?'

A shutter of caution fell into place as he said, 'How do you mean, "odd"?'

'Some people backstage,' said Carole airily, the long-established source of company gossip, 'have mentioned the word "murder".'

'No surprise there,' said Tony.

'What do you mean?'

'Actors are highly superstitious people. They also – hardly surprisingly, given their job – have a tendency to overdramatize things. And a lot of them have acted in many whodunits, in the theatre and on telly. So, given an unnatural death backstage, they're going to be very attracted to the idea that it must be murder. But that's no reason to think it *was* murder. Just a lot of highly strung people letting their imaginations run away with them.'

It was a reasonable reply but did not completely allay Carole's suspicions. 'Have you heard any specific accusations levelled against anyone in the company?'

He thought for a moment about his answer. Was he assessing whether he wanted to land one of his *House/Home* colleagues in trouble? Or was he thinking of a way to exclude himself from suspicion? 'Well,' he said finally, 'the one person Drake Purslow was constantly at odds with was Babs Backshaw.'

'Yes, I kind of got that impression,' said Carole. 'But do you think she would have bothered to go to the trouble of murdering him?'

'Oh, she wouldn't have done it herself,' said the writer. 'Babs never does anything for herself. She has staff to do everything for her.'

Carole and Jude looked at each other, once again sharing the same thought. They had just witnessed how ready Gerald Tarquin was to stay in Babs Backshaw's good books by obeying her every whim.

'Even to commit murder?' asked Carole.

'I'm sure,' Tony replied, 'if she wanted to, she'd find someone to do the job. But I can't really see it. OK, Drake annoyed her when he bawled her out for being unprofessional . . . you know, late for rehearsals, inserting one of her catchphrases from her Netflix show into *House/Home* – that kind of thing. But she's had all kinds of uncharitable things said about her on social media, and it's all been water off a duck's back. She's a tough one, that Babs. It'd take more than a few spats to make her want to murder someone.'

'And,' Carole asked eagerly, 'is there anyone else in the company who might have had a motive for murdering Drake Purslow?'

Tony Grover let out a harsh chuckle. 'Certainly not me, if that's the way your thoughts are straying. It was in my interest, with the prospect of a West End transfer looming, to keep as many of the *House/Home* stage company together as possible. So, I'm not going to go around randomly murdering them, am I?'

'One wouldn't have thought so,' said Jude judiciously. 'On the other hand, if Drake Purslow was being rude about the show he was in, and telling everyone he met that he hated it and couldn't wait till the tour ended . . . well, that wasn't so good for the all-important "word of mouth" you were talking about earlier. Was it?'

Tony Grover now looked decidedly shifty. He changed the direction of the conversation. 'All that concerns me is that this show transfers. And if everyone involved is as bloody useless as the Clincham Theatre management, then it's not going to happen.'

Jude's background in the theatre meant that she was better informed in this area than Carole. 'But surely,' she objected, 'it's not the Clincham Theatre management you should be blaming. Yes, OK, perhaps they could have done a bit more publicity, but *House/Home* wasn't their show. They didn't produce it. During the winter season, Clincham Theatre is always a "receiving house". And here was a show in the last week of its tour, which was already nearly sold out, just on the name and the demographics of Clincham, which supplied a generation who'd grown up on the telly series. Why should they bother investing in more publicity?'

Tony Grover looked beleaguered and said doggedly, 'They've got it in for me.'

'Who? Clincham Theatre?'

'Them and the others.'

'What "others"?'

'The whole bloody establishment! Oh, there are some writers they always make a fuss of. Give them all the theatre awards, bloody knighthoods and all that. But if you're a writer who doesn't fit into that charmed circle, you might as well forget it.'

'Are you going through a rough patch on the work front?' asked Jude sympathetically.

'You could say that.' Jude had known her question would unleash a catalogue of grievances and remembered slights, but she reckoned there was a chance he might divulge some useful information in the tsunami.

'Television's a very fickle business,' the writer began, building up a head of paranoid steam. 'As a medium, it's bloody hard to work for. Somebody once said, "You don't write for television. You *re*write for television." You keep having to do bloody rewrites. It seems like everyone involved in the production has the right to shred your script. And I'd much rather never do any television again than go through all the bloody hassle.

'But – and it's a big "but" – television does pay so much better than virtually anything else. And when the telly money's streaming in, you kind of get used to it. You adjust your lifestyle to the new circumstances. I had a very cushy decade while the *House/Home* series was running. And then it went on a bit with foreign sales and that kind of stuff.

'And new work. Or there should have been new work. You create a successful sitcom, which is in the top-ten viewing figures right through its run, and you'd have thought the writer of that would have been inundated with offers. But no, suddenly they all turn against me.'

Now, there was a real flicker of paranoia in his eye. 'Even the show that's a spin-off from *House/Home* . . . the series that takes Hayley, *my* character, the character who didn't exist before I invented her . . . they take her away from me. Oh, I wrote the pilot for *Some People* . . . they couldn't have started it without my script. But when they get to the series, I'm unceremoniously bumped off the project. Suddenly, my onscreen credit's just "Based on a character created by Tony Grover". And I get paid a pittance. And all those lovely fat script fees are being paid to hacks who know how to structure telly scripts but have never had an original thought in their lives. And I get nothing but a format fee.

'So, I have to find work in other areas of show business, and it's hard. Bit of radio, bit of stage stuff, but none of it pays anything like the telly does. And—'

Carole, having endured enough of this litany of self-pity, interrupted, 'And, of course, another of your stage adaptations was done at Clincham Theatre, wasn't it?'

'Yes. *The Woman in White.*' Once again, he reached out for praise. 'Did you like it?'

'Oh, I didn't see it,' came the withering reply.

'Then why did you mention it?'

Jude took over. 'Because it was during that production, down here, that Ollie Luke died.'

Tony Grover looked shocked by the mention of the name. 'Yes. His girlfriend was in my adaptation. Girl called Rhona Revell. She played the ugly one, Marian Halcombe. Anita, who was here today, played the pretty one, Laura Fairlie. That was another of my shows that had a chance of going into the West End, but again it was screwed up by the Clincham Theatre management.'

Jude was beginning to wonder whether the writer's litany of bad luck might have something to do with his personality. Was it the case, perhaps, that people who'd worked with him once didn't want to repeat the experience?

'You heard about the circumstances of his death?' asked Carole.

'Of course I did.' The tone of the answer made it sound as though it had been a stupid question. Which, Carole reflected, it had been. Still, it had got him on to the subject she wanted to talk about.

'A story like that doesn't just go away,' Tony went on. 'The press were all over it. "Drug Overdose Death of Sitcom Star" – it's the kind of headline the hacks dream of. No one connected with *House/Home* could escape the furore.'

'Were you aware that Ollie had a drug problem?' asked Jude.

'No. But I didn't know much about him. I mean, I saw him on studio days when we were making the series. Not outside work, though. We weren't close.'

'Did you think he was gay?'

'Didn't think much about it. There were rumours around the *House/Home* rehearsal room that he was. People said he got the part of Spike because the director fancied him. But, as I say, I didn't see Ollie socially. Bit of a surprise, though, when I heard through the theatre grapevine that he'd got a girlfriend.'

'Did you meet him with Rhona while you were working on *The Woman in White*?'

'Not during rehearsals, which all happened down here in Clincham. When the show was running, I saw him briefly on the final Friday, the night he saw the show.'

'The day before he died?' asked Carole urgently.

'Yup,' he said, making the word sound totally non-committal. 'Possibly the day he died. I thought he was pronounced dead on the Friday evening.'

Then, suddenly, he looked from one woman to the other. 'Oh, I see what's going on here. You two are playing amateur sleuths, are you?'

'Maybe. A bit,' Jude replied with sheepish charm.

Tony Grover nodded. 'I see. And you're checking out whether there might be any connection between the deaths of Ollie Luke and Drake Purslow?'

'That's exactly what we're doing,' said Carole.

'Ah.' He drained the remains of his Guinness. 'In that case, I'm not sure that I can help you any more.'

'Might you give us a couple more minutes,' suggested Jude coquettishly, 'if we were to buy you another drink?'

He only thought about the offer for a moment. Clearly, from what he had implied, the Grover finances were not in a very healthy state. 'Pint of Guinness,' he said.

'I'll get it,' said Jude, to her neighbour's surprise and gratification. At this pivotal moment, Carole was being allowed to lead the investigation.

'Could we just go back to the question about Ollie Luke and drugs?' she asked.

'If you like,' said Tony Grover nonchalantly.

'You never heard of him being involved with stuff?'

'No. But that didn't mean anything. There was a lot of drug-taking around television in those days. And the actors were very well paid. So, it wouldn't have been surprising news to hear that any of the *House/Home* company had developed a habit.'

'What about you?'

For a moment, he looked affronted, but then seemed to decide it didn't matter. 'Yes, I served my time at the mercy of the needle. That's where too much of my income went. I'm clean now. But it took a while.'

'So, the night Ollie Luke died . . .'

'Yes?'

'Which was, incidentally, the Saturday, not the Friday.'

'All right,' he grudgingly conceded.

'What did you do?'

'Well, I watched my play, didn't I? I watched what I knew to be the last night of the Clincham run, in the hope that it would be one of many last nights and first nights, as the play took off to the West End and Broadway.'

'But . . .?' Carole prompted.

'But' – he grinned without humour – 'that last night turned out to be *the* last night.'

'Ah. And after the last night was over . . .?'

He anticipated her. 'No, I did not join Rhona and the rest of the party going to The Gryphon in Brighton. By then, I was off the drugs and my clubbing days were over.'

'Do you know who went with Rhona in the cab to Brighton?'

'No. I think she may have had friends down from London to see the show, but I didn't meet them, so I can't give you any names.'

'No one else from the company went with her?'

'Don't think so.'

'And do you know which friends of Ollie Luke were in Brighton – you know, the ones who had come down from London with him?'

'No idea.'

At that moment, Jude returned from the bar. She hadn't just got a drink for Tony. On the tray she was carrying, along with the Guinness, were two large glasses of New Zealand Sauvignon Blanc.

Carole had a momentary qualm. They were now well into the afternoon, and she hadn't had any lunch. Should she be drinking large glasses of New Zealand Sauvignon Blanc on an empty stomach, particularly with the prospect at some point of driving the Renault back to Fethering? She decided she should and took a long slurp. As did Jude.

With the neediness of an addict, Tony took a long swallow of his Guinness. Then, aggressively, he said, 'All right, you've bought me the drink. What else do you want to ask about the two deaths?'

'Coming back to Drake's,' asked Jude, 'from the after-show party on the stage, what were the logistics of someone going from there to his dressing room?'

'By "logistics", you mean, was there anything to stop a member of the company from going from the melee onstage up to his dressing room?'

'Exactly.'

'No problem at all. Anyone could have done it. You didn't have to go past Nell on the stage door to get to the dressing rooms.'

'No.'

'And if you're about to ask whether I saw anyone creeping up the dressing-room stairs with murderous intent, the answer is no.'

'I wasn't going to ask that,' Jude asserted.

'Good.'

'Rhona Revell,' said Carole.

'What about her?'

'Did you see anything of her after the production of *The Woman in White* finished?'

'No. I sent her a card of condolence about Ollie. That was the last communication between us.'

'Have you heard anything about what happened to her since then?'

'No. Not really.'

'What does that mean?'

'It means I haven't seen her or spoken to her on the phone, but I did hear a rumour that she had given up the theatre.'

'Ah.'

'Not a bad idea. She wasn't any great shakes as an actor.'

'And you've no idea what she did, where she went or what name she went under?'

'No, no and no,' replied Tony Grover with a degree of satisfaction.

'But I—'

Jude was interrupted by the ringing of Carole's mobile. It was answered instantly.

'Hello?' said Carole.

The voice from the other end said, 'Are you the person who wanted to talk about Ollie Luke's death?'

FIFTEEN

'I went back to my birth name,' she said. 'Katharine Clithero. Known as Katie.'

They were in what had once been a shop in the back streets of Clincham. From the outside, the front window appeared to have been painted over, but it must have been done with a covering that let the light in. The interior was airy and welcoming. The walls were green, bright and lush, not that institutional green that had depressed so many people needing public services over the years. The colourful spines of books on the shelves added to the cheering atmosphere. But for the subject matter of the books, the space could have been the children's section of a library.

On the outside door had been the letters 'DRC'. If Katie hadn't told Carole on the phone, she wouldn't have known they stood for 'Drug Rehabilitation Centre'. She had never given much thought to what a drug rehabilitation centre might look like, but this certainly wasn't it.

'Obviously, I got into this world,' Katie went on, 'because of what happened to Ollie. I was just so appalled by the power of drugs. The fact that one injection could destroy a life . . . I knew I could never get back the only man I ever truly loved, but at least I thought I could do something to stop others from going the same way.'

Katie Clithero was not traditionally attractive. She had mousy hair and slightly pudgy features. Carole and Jude could see why she'd been cast as Marian Halcombe, the 'ugly one' in *The Woman in White*. But there was a directness and honesty in the way her grey eyes instantly engaged with theirs that gave her a kind of magnetism.

'I'm sorry, incidentally,' she said, 'to drag you over here, but I'm manning the phones. Particularly important at weekends – lots of temptations around then for potential addicts.'

'I'm sure there are,' said Carole, sounding very middle-class and disapproving. 'Even somewhere nice, like Clincham.'

'You'd better believe it. Anyway, we see to it that the phonelines are manned twenty-four seven. There's someone upstairs who could take over, but she's only a trainee, so that's why I'm doing it now. So, sorry I couldn't come to see you.'

'It's not a problem,' said Jude. 'We were in Clincham, anyway.'

'Oh God, yes. Were you attending the Babs Backshaw extravaganza at the theatre?'

'Yes. I was there as a volunteer,' said Carole. Realizing that she still had her ID lanyard round her neck, she sheepishly removed it.

'I saw about it in the local paper,' said Katie.

'Do you know Babs Backshaw?' asked Jude.

'Well, I know *of* her, of course. Hard to escape, these days.'

'But have you met her?'

'No.'

'You haven't missed a lot,' said Carole, and for once Jude would have shared her waspishness.

'But I heard Ollie talking about her enough to get a pretty full picture. Ego, ego and more ego. Riding roughshod over everything and everyone. And the more offensive she is, the more the public seem to love her.'

'That about sums it up,' Carole agreed, and went on, 'Did Ollie talk about how he got on with her during the *House/Home* television years?'

'Yes. I think "polite loathing" would be the appropriate description. They both knew they had to find a way of working together, and they saw as little as possible of each other outside work.'

'Hm,' said Carole. 'And what about the rest of the *House/Home* company? Were there any others Ollie didn't hit it off with?'

'Well . . .' Katie began, then pieced things together. 'Oh, I see. You two are trying to work out whether any of the people from the show might have had a hand in Ollie's death. Aren't you?'

'Yes, I'm afraid we are,' Jude admitted. 'I'm sorry. We should have owned up to that straight away.'

'Don't apologize. I've been longing for someone to reopen the case. I know the verdict was accidental death, but I never believed that. I still think Ollie was murdered.'

Carole and Jude exchanged covert looks. This was what they wanted to hear.

Katie Clithero looked at them sharply and made another connection. 'Is it the other recent death that has got you digging up ancient history? That actor, Drake Purslow, are you suggesting he was murdered, too?'

Jude recapitulated the events of the night when she saw the last performance of the *House/Home* stage show, concluding, 'And I know I saw that shoeprint in the blood. Not the complete sole, just the semicircle of the front bit. So, I'm convinced someone else had been in the dressing room with Drake.'

'What happened to the shoeprint?'

'It was effectively erased when Fiona Crampton knelt down on a pile of tissues to check Drake's vital signs. Do you know Fiona Crampton?'

'I know who she is and what she does, but I haven't met her.'

'Not when you were doing *The Woman in White*?' asked Carole.

'No way. The theatre has been through God knows how many changes of management since then. Anyway, though I'm living in the same city, I tend to avoid Clincham Theatre and anything to do with the place.'

'I can understand that,' said Jude empathetically.

'But,' asked Katie, 'do you think Fiona Crampton deliberately tampered with the evidence?'

'Hard to say. It looked like her movements were completely natural – no forethought involved. But if she did do it deliberately, I think she must have known the shoeprint was there before we went into the dressing room.'

'Was the shoeprint from a woman's shoe or a man's?'

'Oh, Katie, I wish I could give you an answer to that. It certainly wasn't a woman's shoe like a pointy-toed stiletto. But these days, almost everyone of every available gender wears trainers. Particularly around the theatre. So, I would have said what I saw was the toeprint of a trainer, which could have belonged to absolutely anyone.'

'And you have particular reason for thinking Drake Purslow's death might be connected with Ollie's?'

Carole and Jude, rather shamefacedly, had to admit that they didn't. 'It's just . . . both connected with the same theatre . . .' was Carole's rather feeble response.

But they were cheered when Katie said, 'I've been thinking about a connection.'

'Really? What?'

'After Ollie's death, I tried to contact most of the *House/Home* company . . . you know, to see whether they had any insight into why it had happened. I was partly afraid that one of them would reveal he really did have a long history of drug-taking while they were doing the show. Though I'm glad to say that didn't happen.

'Anyway, my overtures to most of the company were pretty ineffective. They'd moved on. They weren't much interested in what happened to Ollie . . . and they certainly didn't want to have their media images tarnished by association with someone who'd died of an overdose.

'The one exception was Drake Purslow. I didn't meet him, but he was happy to talk to me on the phone. He was the only one who seemed genuinely shocked by Ollie's death. Shocked and suspicious about it. He couldn't take on board the idea of Ollie dabbling with drugs. I sort of got the impression Drake had been quite protective of Ollie when he started in the telly series. Nothing sinister – just sort of keeping an eye out for him, seeing he didn't get bullied by some of the stronger personalities in the company.'

'Like Babs Backshaw?' Jude suggested.

'Exactly like Babs Backshaw,' Katie agreed. 'Whenever Drake's name came up, Ollie spoke of him with great fondness.'

'So, what are you thinking?' asked Carole.

'I was thinking, if Ollie's killer was someone connected with the telly series, and Drake Purslow ever talked out loud about his suspicions – or even accused someone of the murder – then the perpetrator might well have a reason to silence him before the rumours spread any further.'

Carole nodded in slow admiration. 'I like that idea.'

Jude asked, 'Did you have any contact with Drake while he was here in Clincham for the *House/Home* run?'

'Well, that was strange. I didn't know he was down here. As I said, I try to avoid anything to do with Clincham Theatre. But I did have a text during that week.'

'From Drake?'

'Yes.' Her fingers were busy on her mobile. 'Ah. I thought I hadn't erased it. Says: "Thinking of you and your troubles. Maybe will have something to report soon. Love, Drake."'

'And you immediately thought,' suggested Carole keenly, 'that he was making headway on the investigation into Ollie Luke's death?'

'I'm afraid I didn't immediately think that. Didn't think about it at all. Back then, I was very deep into an investigation with the West Sussex Police. They were closing in on a gang who'd been supplying opioids to schoolkids in Clincham. I couldn't think of anything else. In fact, I'd completely forgotten about Drake's text until you asked whether he'd been in contact recently.'

'But saying he might have "something to report",' Carole insisted, 'what else might he have been reporting to you about?'

'As I say, I didn't really think about it.'

'But now that you *do* think about it, you realize that's what it could have been referring to?'

'I guess so.'

'But,' said Jude, 'it does chime in with your idea about the murderer of Ollie finding out that Drake was on to the truth and killing him to stop him talking.'

'It does, yes.' Katie Clithero sounded suddenly exhausted. Though she wanted to know what had actually happened, digging up that part of her past was stressful.

Jude moved on to something else. 'Katie, were you at Ollie's inquest?'

'Yes, I followed every step of the investigation that I was allowed to.'

'Why do you think the possibility of someone else injecting him with the fatal overdose wasn't raised then? Or maybe it was . . .?'

Katie shook her head. 'Look, I don't want to sound like a conspiracy theorist, but I think the scenario of Ollie injecting himself with the drugs suited the police and the press very well. Someone of Ollie's profile having succumbed to an overdose – good cautionary tale for the police's anti-drugs campaign. And it gave the tabloids plenty of opportunities for self-righteous feature articles. Oh, they loved it.'

'Are you saying you think the police investigation was flawed?' asked Carole eagerly. From her Home Office background, this was an area she knew a bit about.

Katie sighed. 'I might have thought that, but there was no point in going public about it. One bereaved girlfriend wasn't going to have much clout against the massed powers of the establishment.'

The mobile on the desk rang. It was picked up instantly. 'Katie here.' She looked disappointed. 'They rang off.'

She picked up a small walkie-talkie and pressed a button. 'Jay, just had a call from Des. Well, he rang the number but rang off when I answered. Could you give him a call, see if you can get anything out of him?'

'OK,' crackled the response.

'He's on the Red Risk List, so if you don't get through, I'll have to go out to his place and leave you on the phones.'

That got another crackly 'OK'.

Katie Clithero smiled ruefully at her visitors. 'Sorry, I may have to go. One of our high-risk clients. But what else do you want to ask me about Ollie's death?'

'You reckon,' said Carole, 'that someone in The Gryphon Club injected him with the overdose?'

'That's the only thing I can think. From all accounts, it was pretty chaotic in there. Anything could have happened. Thought most likely to have happened in the gents.'

'I did some research on the press coverage at the time.'

'All vile, sanctimonious lies.'

'Yes, it probably was. But you, Katie, were quoted as saying Ollie had never touched drugs.'

'It's true. We'd even talked about it. He admitted he'd had something of an alcohol problem at one point – you know, just after the telly series started, and he couldn't cope with all the media interest. But he said he'd never touched any drug stronger than an aspirin. I remember, because of how he said it. He said he'd never been "brave" enough to take drugs . . . you know, as if it was some failure on his part, kind of being chicken about it.

'Also . . . well, it may sound obvious, but I knew Ollie's body pretty well. And I never saw any sign of needle marks anywhere on it. He'd never injected himself with anything, which was maybe why the single dose had such a terrible effect.'

Carole nodded, and Jude asked, 'Sorry, it's a sensitive area, but we've heard from one or two sources that Ollie might have been gay.'

Katie Clithero was more than ready to answer that one. 'From what he told me, his first sexual experiences were with men . . . well, boys at school, just fumbling around. And I think in his teens he suffered a lot from anxiety about his sexuality. There were rumours around that he got the part of Spike in *House/Home* because the director fancied him. Then the exposure he got from being in a hit telly series prompted a lot of interest from gay men. I think he found it hard to deal with . . . well, I *know* he found it hard to deal with. He told me so.'

'And . . . sorry to ask this . . . but did you ever notice any signs that his sexual interests might lie elsewhere?'

Katie grinned. 'You mean, did I notice in bed?'

'If you like.'

'I've never had sex like it. You know, we just fitted. Two people who were designed solely to provide each other with pleasure. There's absolutely no question when it's that good . . . as I'm sure you know.'

Jude grinned in complicity, and Carole looked rather embarrassed.

'We were just right for each other. When we both got a break in our work schedule, we were going to get married, have kids . . . I've never met anyone else who . . .' Her grey eyes strayed off into impossibilities.

'I'm sorry,' said Jude. Not for the first time, Carole envied her friend's ability to get the tone just right for any situation.

But she had a more urgent need for information. 'I believe, Katie, that you had the unfortunate experience of getting all the way to Brighton before you got news of Ollie Luke's death.'

'Yes, Carole.' She took a long gulp of air to steady herself. 'That was the worst moment of my life. When I saw the police cars and ambulances around the entrance to the club . . .' Again, she ran out of words.

'And do you know,' Carole persisted, 'who Ollie had come down to the South Coast with? There was some talk of "friends" with him, I believe.'

'Maybe. He didn't mention them. We were just so excited to see each other.'

'When he came to see *The Woman in White* on the Friday evening,' asked Jude, 'did he have anyone with him?'

'No. He came on his own.'

'And had that always been the intention?'

'How do you mean, Jude?'

'Presumably, you organized comps for him on the Friday?'

'Yes, of course.'

'I'm sorry,' Carole interposed, 'but what are "comps"?'

'Complimentary tickets.'

'Ah.' There were still some gaps in Carole's theatrical education.

'So, Katie,' Jude resumed, 'did Ollie ask you to reserve one comp for him? Or more?'

'Ah. Good point.' A moment of brain-racking. 'I'm sorry, the rest of that night was so magical that I've forgotten . . . No, no, it's coming back. Yes, he had asked me to get the box office to hold two comps. Then, when he came round backstage after the show, he said he'd come on his own, because his mate had . . . Now, what was the wording he used? He said his mate had "had enough of the bloody theatre and gone to explore Brighton's clubland".'

'Did he give the "mate" a name?' asked Carole.

'Oh God. We are talking quite a few years ago. And a time that I have deliberately tried *not* to remember.' Katie's chubby face screwed up with the effort of recollection. 'Could it have been Gary? No, doesn't sound right. Something like that, though . . . Terry! Yes, I'm pretty sure it was Terry.'

There was a buzz from the walkie-talkie on Katie's desk. She pressed a button. Jay's voice crackled down to her. 'I couldn't get any reply from either Des's mobile or the landline.'

'Oh God.' Katie's hands were already reaching for what looked like a medical bag. 'I must get round to his place. Jay, you're in charge of the phones!'

She looked at Carole and Jude, holding her hands out in an expression of helpless apology. 'I'm sorry. I must get round there. The boy's a serious suicide risk.'

As the shop door closed behind her, the two visitors looked at each other in bewilderment.

'And who the hell is Terry?' asked Jude rhetorically.

SIXTEEN

They seemed to have hit the buffers. They had got the useful information about Drake's text, which certainly could mean they were making headway on the investigation into Ollie Luke's death. But they couldn't follow up with Katie, at least until she had dealt with her addict's emergency.

So, they were sitting in a café called Pico's, feeling despondent. Carole had a black Americano in front of her, and Jude a cappuccino. Jude had swallowed down the residue of her New Zealand Sauvignon Blanc at The Feathers, while Carole had abandoned hers, hardly touched. Both were hungry. It was mid-afternoon. Carole had ordered a cheese salad, Jude a jumbo sausage roll. They had paid for everything at the counter.

'If only,' said Jude, 'we could talk to someone else who was around Clincham Theatre during the run of *The Woman in White*.'

'Didn't you say, that time when Fiona Crampton warned you off further investigation, that one of the stagehands offered to help?'

'Good heavens, you're right! I'd completely forgotten about Mo. He wanted to talk to me after Anita's ceremony but had to go off to a meeting.'

Jude reached into the pocket of her thick woolly cardigan and produced the grubby card he'd given her. She keyed in the number on her phone. A slight tug of annoyance at the corner of her mouth showed she'd got through to a voicemail message.

'Mo,' she said, 'This is Jude.' She tailored her message to something that would sound innocuous in a crowded café. 'Remember we met in Fiona Crampton's office, and you said you'd be happy to help my research work. Well, I think I'm near to a breakthrough. So, if you could ring me back as soon as possible, that'd be great. Thanks.'

She ended the call and looked ruefully at her neighbour. 'Who knows whether he's got anything new. But he did seem to share my suspicions about Drake Purslow's death.'

'Well, we'll just have to wait till he rings.'

'Yes.' Jude didn't sound happy about the prospect. A sudden thought. 'What about your friend Nonie? She seems to be a walking encyclopaedia of everything that has ever happened at Clincham Theatre.'

'She is. And more than ready to spill any available beans. Good idea.' Carole did the routine with her phone. She too grimaced when she got through to a message. She asked Nonie to call her back. 'Best I can do. I don't have a clue where she lives. Obviously, I can ask her stuff when we're next working together on the archive, but that's not till Wednesday.'

'We need something before then.' Jude sounded uncharacteristically tense. 'I just have a feeling that we're very near to solving this crime, and at this point it's very frustrating to have to delay our investigation.'

'Couldn't agree more.' Carole's self-critical expression changed to something more serene. 'Oh. There is more than one "walking encyclopaedia" of Clincham Theatre.'

'Really?'

Carole was already scrolling through numbers on her mobile. She found what she was looking for and pressed the 'call' button.

'Hello,' she said when it was answered. 'Myrna, this is Carole Seddon speaking.'

In Pico's, the cheese salad and jumbo sausage roll were delivered to an empty table. Carole and Jude were hot-footing it to St Clare's Hospital. To be specific, to the café in the private wing.

Despite her age, Myrna Crace again looked effortlessly elegant, in a burgundy suit with a fur collar. She insisted on getting coffee for them, the same order as the ones that were rapidly cooling on a table in Pico's.

Myrna had a very steady hand as she brought the tray back from the counter. Once all three were seated, she said, 'I presume, Carole, that you got involved in the Babs Backshaw debacle?'

'Yes. I volunteered.'

'Huh. Thank heavens that Eric was not alive to see that happen to his precious theatre.'

'But surely,' suggested Carole, 'he must have got involved in fundraisers over the years.'

'Of course he did. But they were fundraisers organized by the theatre management in aid of Clincham Theatre, and given sufficient time for proper planning. They weren't spur-of-the-moment sideshows set up by some publicity-hungry actress.'

Jude got the feeling that Myrna Crace was of the generation that would only use the word 'actor' to describe those of masculine gender.

'The current management is too soft,' pronounced the member of Clincham Theatre royalty. 'Lazlo, of course, is never there, and Fiona just keeps caving in to the demands of actors and directors. The girl has no backbone.'

Jude, who had met her, thought Fiona Crampton showed considerable backbone. But, clearly, Myrna Crace had more demanding standards.

'Eric would never have agreed to allowing anything like that tug-of-war being put on without proper planning. The insurance for suddenly opening the premises on a Sunday at short notice . . . it must have been ruinous. Then paying extra weekend shifts for the staff . . . Why on earth did Fiona agree to it?'

Carole attempted some explanation. 'Babs Backshaw had announced it on social media.'

'And what does that have to do with anything?' came the frosty response.

'She posted that the theatre management was backing it because it was for a children's hospice charity.'

'But she hadn't asked the theatre management.'

'I agree. She hadn't. Babs Backshaw has a huge following on social media, though. They haven't a clue about the rights or wrongs of the situation. All they know is that Babs has told them she's setting up a charity tug-of-war at Clincham Theatre. If the management pulled the plug on the thing, then they'd come across as spoilsports who want to deny money to a children's hospice. That kind of adverse publicity would have been very harmful to Clincham Theatre's profile.'

'A theatre's profile,' Myrna protested, 'should be based on the quality of the plays it puts on, not the posturing of minor actresses.'

'Well, maybe . . .' said Carole cautiously.

'Anyway, it happened,' said an emollient Jude, hoping that the conversation could be moved away from the subject of Babs Backshaw's perfidy.

'It wouldn't have happened if Eric was still running the place,' said Myrna Crace definitively. She couldn't resist making that statement but was then content to move the conversation on. 'Carole, you said on the phone you wanted to talk about Drake Purslow's death.'

'Yes. And, well, also about Ollie Luke's death.'

'That's not a name I've heard for a long time.'

'But you know who we mean?'

'Oh, certainly. Actor who was in the original television show on which the rubbish stage play was based – the one that was in the theatre last week.'

'You thought it was rubbish?' asked Jude.

'Yes. Did you see it?'

'Mm.'

'And didn't you think it was rubbish?'

Jude had always found it hard to condemn the work of fellow actors, so she replied, 'I didn't think it was very well written.'

'Huh.' Myrna was more forceful in her opinions. 'No sense of structure, and a load of innuendo which, if it belonged anywhere, was on a lavatory wall.'

'I saw a recording of the original television show,' said Carole, ingratiating herself, 'and I shared your opinion of the writing, Myrna.'

Her view was acknowledged by a gracious smile. 'Drake Purslow certainly thought it was rubbish,' Myrna went on.

'Did you see him while he was working down here on the stage show?' asked Jude.

'Oh yes. Drake had been in quite a few productions here for Eric, you know, before he got seduced away by the television money. Gave a very fine Aufidius in Eric's *Coriolanus*, and a lovely Trigorin in *The Seagull*. Drake was an excellent actor, very truthful.'

'So, when did you see him?' asked Carole.

'On the Thursday of the run. We met for tea in the Copper Kettle on Clincham High Street. Just to chat over old times.'

'And how did he seem?'

'As he always had done, Jude. Enormously charming.'

'Yes, that's how I remember him.'

'Oh, you knew him?'

'Worked with him way back.'

'So, you're in the business?'

'Was. Very firmly was.'

'What do you do now?'

'I'm a healer.'

'Oh?'

Carole was slightly miffed that Myrna Crace seemed to regard healing as a perfectly normal profession. Also, she didn't think she was getting her fair share of the conversation. 'When you met, did Drake Purslow talk about any threats to him?'

'Threats? What kind of threats?'

'There is a view among some people at Clincham Theatre that he died as a result of foul play.'

'Murder, do you mean?'

'Yes.'

'That wouldn't surprise me at all.' Myrna's calmness matched her words.

'You mean you think he was murdered?'

'No. I mean I think it likely that people at Clincham Theatre might suggest he was murdered. Actors and actresses – everyone connected with the theatre, in fact – have a strong tendency to overdramatize.'

Exactly what Tony Grover had said.

'So, did he talk about any threats?' Carole persisted.

'Not threats, no. But we did talk about death.'

'Why?'

Myrna Crace spread her hands wide. 'When you get to my age, death comes into a lot of conversations.'

'But Drake wasn't worried about anyone wanting to kill him?'

'No. He did talk about how much he hated being in the production, how he couldn't wait till the tour ended.'

'So,' asked Jude, 'there was no chance of him going with the show if it went to the West End?'

'Absolutely none. He loathed every minute he spent doing it. But I don't know who was spreading rumours about it going to the West End. There was no chance at all of a show like that transferring.'

'There's an age group who would have been familiar with the television series.'

'Yes, but not enough to fill a West End theatre for any length of time. Do you know how much it costs to put on even a modest show there these days? Eric had some very successful productions that transferred, but the whole business has changed totally since those days. Now it's got to be a film or television star . . . or some musical based on a movie. A show like *House/Home* would have no chance at all.'

'Tony Grover,' said Carole, 'seemed to think a transfer was quite likely.'

'Writers are all fantasists,' said Myrna contemptuously.

'So,' Carole pressed on, 'did Drake Purslow talk to you about any major personality clashes he had during the rehearsals and tour of the *House/Home* tour?'

'Only with Babs Backshaw. He said it wasn't in his nature to celebrate anyone's death, but in her case, he'd make an exception.'

'That's quite strong.'

'I was quite surprised by it. Drake was normally the most generous of men, very courteous to his fellow actors. But she had clearly got up his nose.'

'And do you think he got up her nose to an equal extent?'

'I should think that's entirely possible. Apparently, he didn't keep his views on the professional shortcomings of Babs Backshaw to himself.'

'Didn't he?' came the meaningful response from Carole.

'If we can go back to Ollie Luke's death . . .' suggested Jude.

'Of course.'

'Was your husband still running the theatre then?'

'No, he had just retired and wasn't taking it well. He was supposed still to have a "consultancy" role, but the new director showed no signs of wanting to consult him. By then, Eric wasn't well and was getting very depressed about everything. You know, he didn't think he'd achieved much in his life, wasn't going to leave any kind of legacy. Which was, of course, complete nonsense, given the amount he'd done for Clincham Theatre, but you can't argue with a depressive.'

'Did he see the production of *The Woman in White*?'

'Yes, we were there the last night.'

'The Saturday? The night Ollie Luke died?'

'Yes. Though, of course, we didn't hear about it till the Sunday morning.'

'What did Eric think of the production?' asked Jude.

'He hated it. Said the adaptation needed at least two more drafts to make it vaguely actable. Wondered if anyone on the management side had actually read the script before it went into rehearsal. He blamed the artistic director who'd taken over from him.'

'That wasn't Lazlo, was it?'

'Good God, no. After Eric's long tenure, Clincham Theatre changed artistic directors like Premier League football teams change managers. No, I'm afraid Eric wasn't a good loser. He thought everything at the theatre had run down since he retired. No discipline at rehearsals, stage crew constantly changing their rosters. He thought Clincham Theatre was going to hell in a handcart.'

'How did he react to the news of Ollie Luke's death?'

'Badly. Eric was very morbid by then, thought he wasn't long for this life . . . which sadly proved all too true. He described Ollie Luke's death from an overdose as a symptom of the malaise that affected all theatre and as "another nail in his coffin".'

'But Eric hadn't worked with Ollie, had he?'

'No. He just thought it was symptomatic of the way things were going wrong in the theatre. Not just Clincham – theatre everywhere. Regional rep was virtually gone by then. Eric went on about young actors not "learning their craft". Coming straight out of drama school and getting parts on television, where they just mumbled. He complained there were no actors left who knew how to project and fill a theatre with their voices. Thank goodness he didn't live to see the time when almost all stage actors are miked, as they are nowadays. It would have broken his heart, though it was already pretty much broken.

'So, the death of Ollie Luke, by an overdose of drugs, just seemed to Eric to be another symptom of the decay of the theatrical values which he had grown up with.'

'Had Eric even met Ollie Luke?'

'I don't think so. Though they may have met through Johnny Warburton.'

'The Johnny Warburton who's currently in this hospital,' asked Jude, 'recovering from a stroke?'

'Yes, that's why I'm here. I've just been to visit him.'

'And . . .?' Jude posed the question delicately.

Myrna Crace rotated her wrists in a gesture of uncertainty. 'I don't know. He was certainly very chatty, but then he always has been. The day Johnny Warburton stops gossiping will be the day . . .' She tried to banish the thought. 'He didn't look great to me.'

'Did you see Anita Harcourt?' asked Jude. 'She said she was hoping to have time to pay him a visit.'

'Yes. She was just leaving when I got to Johnny's room.'

Carole reminded Myrna that she said her husband might have met Ollie Luke through Johnny Warburton.

'Yes. Eric and Johnny were great mates. Started out their theatrical careers around the same time. Both initially thought they were actors, then saw that there were a lot more talented actors out there and turned to directing. Where both found their métier. Then Johnny got seduced away from the theatre by the television money, and they didn't see so much of each other after that.'

'We're presuming that Johnny Warburton is' – Carole thought the word 'homosexual' might sound a bit stuffy in theatrical company, so she dared to say – 'gay?'

'God, yes.' Myrna chuckled. 'Flamboyantly gay. Embarrassingly gay, at times. So gay that when he came out, Gay Lib asked him to go back in again.'

Jude joined the chuckle. Carole didn't feel sufficiently uninhibited to do so.

At that moment, Jude's mobile rang. Checking the screen, she asked if they'd mind her taking the call in private and moved to a corridor outside the café. Carole, as she so often – and so often mistakenly – did, assumed it was one of her lovers.

In fact, it was Mo, returning her call.

'Thank you for getting back to me.'

'No problem. Sorry I couldn't talk after the ceremony.'

'You remember we talked about our shared suspicions over Drake Purslow's death?'

'Of course.'

'Well, I think my friend Carole and I might be making some progress there.'

'Good. I've been making a bit of progress on that front, too.'

Jude didn't follow up on that. Be better for them to meet up and share their findings.

'Are you still at the theatre, Mo?'

'Yes. Tidying up the mess left by the crowds at Babs Backshaw's bloody tug-of-war.' He sounded suitably put-upon.

'And are any of the *House/Home* company still around?'

'I think most of them have pissed off back to London. Well, Tony Grover . . . if you count him as one of the *House/Home* company . . . he's probably in The Feathers.'

'And Gerald Tarquin?'

'Gerry? I don't know if he's still around, but if he is, he'll probably be in The Feathers too, commiserating with Tony about how badly the world's treated them both.'

'Well, look . . . Are you still up for finding out what happened to Drake Purslow?'

'Of course, I am.'

'Would you be able to join me and my friend Carole in The Feathers in about an hour?'

'Sure I would.'

If she hadn't been 'on a case', Carole might have been inhibited by being left alone with Myrna Crace. But, as it was, she felt justified in continuing the interrogation. 'What seems to be hard to find out is who Ollie Luke was with in The Gryphon Club that Saturday night.'

Myrna shrugged her elegant shoulders. 'I'm afraid I have no idea.'

'Someone connected with *The Woman in White* company?' Carole suggested, only realizing what a stupid question it had been when Myrna answered.

'It couldn't have been any of them. They didn't go to Brighton until after the show had come down. By which time Ollie Luke was probably already dead. I remember how terrible I thought it must have been for his girlfriend. She was an actress called Rhona Revell.'

Carole didn't think there was much point in revealing how much more she and Jude now knew about the actress in question. Instead, she said, 'That Saturday night, after the performance of *The Woman in White*, did you and Eric go backstage?'

'Yes. Eric wouldn't have forgiven himself if he hadn't "gone round". If the cast members knew he was in for the show, it would have been very bad form for him not to have said a few congratulations to the company.'

'Though, from what you say about Eric's reaction to the show, he was in no mood for congratulations.'

'That's not the point. The actors and actresses have just given a performance. They're exhausted, and the fact that the show was dreadful may not be their fault. With *The Woman in White*, it was the script and the direction that made it such a dreadful experience – mainly the script. You can't blame the actors. No, in the theatre, you always go round and tell them they were *marvellous*.'

'But Eric didn't know any of the actors.' Carole was getting a bit confused by this lesson in theatre protocol.

'All the more reason to tell them they were *marvellous*.'

'Ah.' She managed to make it sound as if she understood. Then she looked at her watch, and an expression of panic took over her face. 'Oh Lord,' she said, 'I'm out of time!'

'I beg your pardon?' Myrna was justifiably confused.

'My car. The Renault. It's in the theatre car park, and we've been here much longer than I expected we'd be.' Carole leapt to her feet and rushed off. 'Sorry! I must put more money in or repark!'

Myrna Crace looked mildly surprised. She didn't know Carole well enough to be aware of her paranoid terror of infringing any kind of legal requirement.

As Carole rushed to the car park, through the unforecast rain, she had another worry. Gulliver had now been shut up in High Tor for far too long. If he had an 'accident', he would be at least as embarrassed as his owner.

As she ran along, Carole Seddon silently bemoaned the logistical problems attendant on being an amateur sleuth.

Jude returned from her phone call, puzzled to see Myrna sitting alone.

'Your friend went off to extend the parking charge on her car.'

'Ah.' Jude knew her neighbour well enough to regard that as characteristic behaviour. 'Sorry to have had to leave you. That call was from Mo.'

'The stagehand?'

'Right. I think he's going to be very helpful in our investigation. Useful to have an insider at the theatre.'

'I'm sure it is.'

'What were you and Carole talking about?'

'I was trying to explain to her the theatrical obligation to "go round" to see the cast after a show.'

Jude giggled. 'I bet Carole didn't get it.'

'No, I don't think she did.'

'And you were talking of you and Eric "going round" after seeing *The Woman in White*?'

'Exactly that. It was a bit of a chore, but Eric insisted it had to be done. Mildly humiliating for him, I'm afraid. None of the actors had a clue who he was. They had no idea about his connection with Clincham Theatre and the huge amount he had achieved there.'

'It must have been awful for him.'

'It was. Mind you, the backstage crew were pleased to see him. Obviously, they'd worked together a lot. Talking to them cheered him up a bit. Eric always made a point of keeping good relations with the permanent stage crew. As a director, you cross them at your peril. So, not for the first time, that evening Eric listened patiently to the whinges of the head of stage.'

'So, what would the head of stage be whingeing about?'

'You name it. Heads of stage can always find something to whinge about. It goes with the territory. Some lighting man misdirecting a follow spot, some actor fluffing his lines and giving the wrong cue . . . the list continues. That evening, after *The Woman in White*, it was, inevitably, about the changed working practices the new artistic director had brought in.'

'What sort of things?'

And Myrna Crace told Jude something she hadn't been expecting to hear.

SEVENTEEN

Myrna had taken them up in the lift to the relevant floor. At the nurses' station, she introduced them and asked if it was possible for Carole and Jude to see Johnny Warburton.

The nurse grimaced. 'Well, he's not very strong, and he has already had two visitors this afternoon.'

'But he does thrive on gossip,' Myrna pointed out.

'And how!' The nurse grinned. 'I can't see that two more visitors are going to make much difference . . . given the state he's in. Go on, then. But no more than two of you.'

'I'll just introduce them,' said Myrna, 'and be on my way.'

Johnny Warburton was not a man to allow being hospitalized to curb his natural flamboyance. He wore scarlet silk pyjamas, with a yellow and red cravat at the neck. The left-hand side of his face sagged a little with the effects of the stroke, which made his voice thin and slurred. Since he was lying down, it was impossible to tell how much his general mobility had been compromised.

'My darlings!' he cried when Myrna had left. 'What a pleasure for a gent of my age to be greeted by two such paragons of pulchritude!'

Jude grinned and Carole looked embarrassed.

'The lovely Myrna said you two were avid consumers of the old theatrical goss, and let me tell you there is no more comprehensive and malicious source of goss than yours truly.'

Jude recognized the kind of character she was dealing with. Johnny Warburton had an image of a flamboyant gay to maintain and, as a result, he came across, quite deliberately, as a stereotype. That was his style, dated and very unlike most gay men Jude knew, whose sexual tastes would never be guessed unless they were actually asked about them.

She knew she was feeling more at ease in this high-camp

milieu than her neighbour, so she directed the conversation. 'We actually wanted to talk to you about the death of Drake Purslow.'

'Ah. Lovely man. Lovely actor. Very serious. Far too serious for the work I did with him. I'm not saying he wasn't good. His Mr Whiffen was perfection, but it wasn't what he really wanted to do. Still, he was in that old financial bind actors get into. He needed the telly money, because of . . . oh, usual actors' problems – cashflow, divorce and all the rest.

'Then he got in with that little sourpuss Imogen Wales. Not an actress ever to be accused of cracking a smile. Still, horses for courses, eh? Imogen Wales would not be to my taste – and not just for the obvious reason. I do have many women friends – a positive coterie, darlings! My own little harem of fag hags. One of them was in the show. Ashley Maxted – lovely girl.

'Replaced Dani Simpkins. Dear Dani, got life so wrong. Tried to work on the principle of "Eat, drink and be merry", but forgot about the eating and the being merry. But I do love my fag hags, you know. And they adore me. I'd be lost without them. They're where I get most of the goss from, you know.'

'Getting back to Drake Purslow . . .'

'Yes. Poor angel. And to die in that way. Brained by Mr Whiffen's hated prop, the computer, the thing he had to lug around with him for all those endless series of *House/Home*. Poor love, he deserved better.'

Carole finally found her voice. 'But, Mr Warburton—'

'Johnny, please, Johnny. Johnny to everyone, from the King to a rent boy.'

'Fine. Johnny, did you hear any rumours about Drake Purslow's death not being natural?'

'And where, darling, might I hear rumours when I'm stuck in here? First few days after the stroke, I was pretty well out of everything. And when I was well enough to see people, a couple of the Clincham Theatre permanent staff came to see me. But did any of that selfish *House/Home* lot, who owe me everything for the way their careers developed . . . did any of them come to see me? A rhetorical question, by the way. They did not, not one of them till dear Anita this afternoon. She always did have more heart, more empathy than the rest of them put together. So, no, I haven't heard any rumours about . . . what was it you said . . . Drake's death "not being natural"? Because I haven't heard any rumours about anything. Stuck here with all these bloody tubes. And they've yet to invent the tube I really want – one that supplies me with an intravenous drip of theatrical gossip.'

Jude tried to get him back on track. 'We're talking about the possibility of Drake having been murdered, Johnny.'

'Ah.' A new caution came into his lopsided face.

'And,' Carole added, 'his murder being in some way related to the murder of Ollie Luke.'

That silenced Johnny Warburton. Finally, in a smaller voice, he asked, 'Do you have any proof that Ollie Luke was murdered?'

'Not exactly proof. Suspicions, though. And maybe some circumstantial evidence.'

'Hm. Who have you got this information from?'

'Various people,' said Carole.

'Anita Harcourt, mostly,' said Jude.

'Ah.' There was a cautious silence. 'The fact is that I have to be a bit wary about this subject.'

'Why?'

'I don't really want there to be a police investigation into that period of my life.'

'Why not?' asked Carole.

He didn't answer the question, instead asking, 'Did Anita talk at all about my casting methods?'

Carole was happy to let Jude respond to this question. 'She did suggest that you had an eye for a good-looking young man.'

The director erupted into spluttery laughter. 'I bet she didn't say "good-looking young man". "Pretty boy" – that was what she said, wasn't it?'

'Yes, it was.'

A little chuckle, then, 'I was rather badly behaved back then. But television in those days, one could get away with . . . I was going to say "murder", but in the circumstances, I don't think I will. I will say "one could have a field day" – a rather more sedate expression . . . and I've had some fun in fields in my time. But in the world of telly, I was in a position of power. I had in my gift the possibility of awarding someone a very lucrative series contract, which could lead to untold riches.

'And there were plenty of pretty boys around keen to take that gift – most of them not too scrupulous about what they might be expected to give in return. I was, back then, like a child in a sweet shop. I could sample any of the goods on display. And I'm not going to apologize for the fact that I took full advantage of that licence. The history of the casting couch is a long one, and even in these days of everyone being po-faced and all "Me Too" about everything, it still gets used as much as ever it did.

'Anyway, as I say, I am not going to apologize for anything I did. To my mind, apology is as stupid and worthless as regret. I don't give houseroom to either of them.'

The long speech seemed to have tired him. He reached for a glass of water on the bedside table. His hand trembled in a juddering motion. Jude lifted the glass to his lips, and he drank gratefully.

Carole didn't feel inclined to give him a break. 'So, you admit that the actor who played Spike in the pilot of *House/Home* was cast on his looks alone?'

'Yes, of course he was. Can't remember his name now but, God, he was gorgeous.'

'Just couldn't act,' Jude suggested.

'Yes. That was a minor drawback. Mind you, I cast his replacement on his looks, too.' There was a note of pride in this admission.

'Ollie Luke?'

'Yes. God, he was gorgeous, too. A bit slow to catch on to what my intentions towards him were. And most upset when he did finally work it out. A very confused young man.'

'So, did you go to bed with him?' asked Jude.

'No. God, I tried to get him to agree. But he really didn't want to. And I've never been into forcing myself on people. Gentle coercion, perhaps, but never more than that. For me, a major attraction of sex is complicity, the fact that the two people involved are doing it because they both want to.'

'I'd go along with that,' said Jude.

Carole said nothing.

'And, of course, I cast Gerry Tarquin for his looks, too. And I'm glad to say he proved more compliant than Ollie. As the original Spike had been.'

'What was the original Spike's name?' asked Carole.

'Do you know, I don't remember. Isn't that awful of me?' It was hard to know whether or not he was lying. He went on, chuckling at his own callousness. 'Maybe Malcolm . . .? No, that's not right. I can't remember. Water under the bridge, eh? Or ships that pass in the night? Or ships that go under the bridge in the night? The right metaphor is in there somewhere, fighting to get out.'

Carole's inquisition continued. 'Did either of the relationships – with the original Spike or with Gerald Tarquin – last long?'

'God, no. I wasn't into anything that lasted long. Too many other goodies in the sweet shop.'

Jude asked, 'And did the relationships end with bad feeling? On either side?'

'Gerry rather cut up rough. But that was complicated – lots of conflicting emotions round the place. Not my emotions – theirs. Gerry had seen me coming on to Ollie Luke, and I think he rather fancied a bit of that.'

'You mean he fancied Ollie?'

'Yes. He was a very jealous boy, Gerry. Didn't like to see me looking at anyone else. And he was always hanging around Ollie. Hoping his luck would change, perhaps. But I think Ollie was working out in his mind, very slowly – he did everything very slowly – that he really fancied women. A tragic loss to the gay community, but not the first time things have worked out that way.'

'So, what happened?' asked Jude.

Johnny's shoulders made an approximation of a shrug. 'Life moved on. Pretty boys become less pretty with time. And then a major road accident is not going to improve a pretty boy's looks, is it?'

'No.' Carole and Jude exchanged meaningful looks. Then Carole turned the beady focus of her pale blue eyes, through her rimless glasses, back on to Johnny Warburton. 'Do you think that Drake Purslow was killed by the same person who killed Ollie Luke?'

'I would say it's a strong possibility, yes.' The camp posturing was gone. The director had become deadly serious.

'Because the killer worked out that Drake knew he'd killed Ollie?'

'Again, I'd say yes. But I should point out that it's only very recently that I've come to these conclusions.'

'How do you mean?'

'It was only after I heard news of Drake's death that I considered the possibility of a connection.'

'But why did you think there was any foul play involved?'

'Because of something Nell told me. Do you know who I mean by Nell?'

'Yes,' said Carole, proud of her newly found Clincham Theatre contacts. 'The stage door keeper.'

'Exactly. Well, apparently she went up to Drake Purslow's dressing room with Fiona Crampton and the person who first found his body.'

'That was me, actually,' said Jude.

'Oh, really?' But he didn't pause to comment. 'Nell said, when she got up to Drake's dressing room, she clearly saw part of a shoeprint in the blood, so she knew someone else had been there when – or immediately after – he'd been killed.'

Carole and Jude both felt stupid. Why hadn't either of them thought to talk to Nell?

'Apparently,' Johnny went on, 'Fiona wiped off the shoeprint when she checked Drake for vital signs. Whether that was a deliberate act . . .'

'If it was deliberate,' said Jude, 'it was just to prevent unnecessary trouble for the theatre. I don't think Fiona had anything to do with the murder.'

Johnny Warburton agreed with her on that. He sighed. 'It comes down to love, I suppose. Or desire. Most things do. You want something, you've wanted it all your life. It could be a person, it could be a career move, it could be anything. And you think you have it in your grasp – and it's snatched away. To someone with a certain kind of temperament, that can be devastating. Lead to all kinds of violent repercussions – even murder.'

A sudden shudder ran through his crippled body, and he let out a gasp of pain. 'Could you call the nurse, please!' he managed to say.

'Obvious, really, wasn't it?' said Carole, as they left the overheated comfort of St Clare's private wing for the chilly outdoors.

'Maybe.'
'Oh, come on, Jude, it is. Couldn't be clearer.'
'Maybe not,' said Jude.
'"Terry" and "Gerry" do sound very alike,' said Carole.

EIGHTEEN

Jude insisted they got drinks first. Each armed with a large New Zealand Sauvignon Blanc, the two women approached their quarry.

Tony Grover sat in exactly the same place as they had left him only an hour or so before. Once again, there was a half-finished pint of Guinness in front of him. But for The Feathers efficient empty-glass-clearing policy, the record of his drinking would be stretched out on the table. The other two were also on the Guinness. Mo gave a nod of complicity to Jude as the two women approached. 'Come on,' he said. 'Make room for my friends.'

Tony Grover was at the glassy-eyed stage of drunkenness that hardly notices new arrivals and departures. Gerald Tarquin said, in his impeccable public school accent, 'I know we met earlier, but I'm frightfully sorry, I've forgotten your names.'

Carole and Jude re-identified themselves.

'Hope you enjoyed the tug-of-war,' he said.

'It was all a bit chaotic,' Jude ventured.

'Well, that's Babs for you.' Gerald Tarquin chuckled. 'Everything's seat-of-the-pants with her. When they created Babs Backshaw, they broke the mould.'

'Maybe.' The actor got Carole's beady eyes focused on him. 'You'd do anything for her, wouldn't you, Gerald?'

He took the question in the spirit of light joshing. 'She's a great girl, and when you've worked on a telly series with someone, you do get close. What's more, Babs hasn't been spoiled by all the success she's had. You know, she's gone on to Hollywood and all that, but she's still in touch with friends like me who, you know, haven't been nearly as successful as she has. She just knows I'm there for her when she needs me.'

'So, I go back to my question: would you do anything Babs Backshaw asked you to do for her?'

'Well, yes. Up to a point.'

'Up to which point?'

'I'd do anything reasonable she asked, yeah.'

'She and Drake Purslow didn't get on, did they?'

'No, all right, they didn't. It was a generational thing. Drake was always twenty years older than most of us, and when we were doing the series, that was fine. But when we got back together to rehearse the stage show, he seemed to have aged a great deal. Become a bit of an old woman, in fact. Talked a lot about the "sanctity" of theatre. So, it was inevitable there would be clashes with a free spirit like Babs Backshaw.'

'Hm.' Carole was rather enjoying running the conversation. She had a sense of the denouement drawing close. She took a confident swallow of Sauvignon Blanc before resuming. 'Did Drake Purslow hear you talking about Ollie Luke's death?'

'What?' Gerald Tarquin was really taken aback. 'What's Ollie got to do with anything?'

'I think Ollie's got to do with a lot of things. A lot to do with Johnny Warburton, at one stage. And a lot to do with you, too, Gerald.'

The public school gloss was off. He just looked very sullen. 'I don't know what you're talking about.'

'I think you do. You were the friend with whom Ollie Luke came down to Brighton for that weekend, the weekend on which he died.'

'What if I was?' came the truculent response.

'And you,' Carole pressed on relentlessly, 'were in The Gryphon Club with Ollie the night he died.'

'No, I wasn't!' Gerald protested. 'And if you're suggesting I had anything to do with Ollie's death, you're way off the mark. That evening, I was furious with Ollie. I didn't want to be with him. I kept well clear of him that evening.'

'But you were—'

Jude interrupted Carole, who looked at her friend with aggrieved amazement. 'It was because of the girl, wasn't it?'

'What girl?' But the feeble way he said it told Jude she was on the right track.

'Rhona Revell,' she said. 'Or, if you want her real name, it's Katie Clithero. It was because of her, wasn't it, Gerald?'

'Yes,' he replied, and he launched into his confessional. He must have had a good few drinks on top of the spliffs to be so self-revelatory in a pub. On the other hand, a crowded pub on a

Sunday afternoon is a pretty good place to share secrets. Nobody can hear anything that's being said at the next table.

'Yes,' Gerald Tarquin repeated, 'it was the girl. The fact is, I loved Ollie. Loved him from the moment I first met him in the *House/Home* rehearsal room. I knew that Johnny Warburton had his eye on him, too, and that made me insanely jealous. I wanted him all to myself.

'And Ollie liked me. He was prepared to be my friend, but he didn't want anything more from the relationship. We hung around a lot together, though. I kept hoping that his attitude to me would change, and sometimes things looked hopeful. Ollie was very confused by the whole business of his sexuality.

'But then he met the girl. Suddenly, he can't think about anything else. He's constantly texting her. Thank God she wasn't in London much, rehearsing some show down here. Anyway, Ollie was insistent that he came down to see her in the show, and equally insistent I came with him.

'I see the weekend as either make or break. If, as he claims, he really is in love with this woman, then I'm off. I'm not going to hang around being constantly rejected. On the Friday night, while he's seeing her show, I cruise Brighton's gay bars, trying to make Ollie jealous. But when he phones from Clincham the next morning, he's so full of the wonderful night he spent with *her* that I know I'm on a hiding to nothing. And I finally know that I'm never going to get what I want.

'So, when I get a text from Ollie later in the day, saying he's going with some people to The Gryphon Club that evening and he looks forward to seeing me there, and Rhona will be joining him after her show comes down, I make the firm decision that wherever I go that evening, it won't be The Gryphon Club. I end up in a shabby bar, where I make a totally unsuitable pick-up, one of a long series that I have regretted over the years.

'So, if you're looking for someone to pin Ollie's murder on and you think it's me, then you couldn't be more wrong.'

Carole looked a little crestfallen, and her mood was not improved when Jude said, 'No, Gerald, I'm not trying to pin it on you. But, Mo, do you mind if I ask you a few questions?'

'No,' he replied coolly. 'If it helps you find who killed Ollie Luke, question away.'

'Well, it couldn't be you, could it?'

'No.'

'Because you were working backstage that night on *The Woman in White* at Clincham Theatre.'

'That's right.'

'And the party from Clincham Theatre didn't leave in their cabs until after the show had come down, by which time Ollie Luke was almost definitely already dead.'

'Exactly,' Mo agreed, smiling serenely.

'You know, Carole and I have just been to see Johnny Warburton in St Clare's Hospital.'

'Really?'

'You know who I mean by Johnny Warburton?'

'Of course I do. He was the director of *House/Home*, telly version and stage, who unfortunately had a stroke on the Monday the show was due to open.'

'Absolutely right. And had you ever met him before?'

'Not to my knowledge.'

'No?' Jude smiled and then said, almost coyly, 'Let me tell you a little story.'

'I came here to have a drink with mates, not to listen to stories.'

'Indulge me.' When she turned on the full charm, Jude could be very persuasive. 'We all know about actor's ambition, don't we? Well, there was once a young actor, who was no great shakes at the actual acting but was very good-looking, attractive to both men and women. And somehow he met a gay television director who found him very attractive and who, as it happened, was about to cast the pilot of a major sitcom series. And, for some reason, he gave this young actor a part in the pilot. The young actor was ecstatic – all his dreams had come together. He was going to be a telly star.

'Everything looked set fair. But – oh dear – the people who make such decisions in television didn't like the young man's acting and demanded the part – Spike the character was called – should be recast for the series.

'Humiliation and fury for the young man involved. And that fury grows over the years and is focused on . . . who? Well, obviously, the actor who took over the part of Spike, the actor who realized all the dreams the rejected actor had nurtured.

'The rejected actor had other bad luck. A car crash sent him through the windscreen, scarring his face. He was no longer even pretty. He stayed in the theatre but no longer as an actor. He had to reconcile himself to working backstage as part of the crew.

'Then, one Friday evening, he sees, in the theatre where he's working, the actor who's stolen his dreams, the actor who's ruined his life. And the fury that has been building up for so long demands to find expression.

'The actor – now stagehand – finds out where his target is going on the Saturday night and fixes with the very slapdash head of stage to be let off his Saturday night shift. He goes earlier in the evening to Brighton and finds his quarry in The Gryphon Club . . .'

Jude looked across at the black-clad figure. 'How'm I doing?'

Mo's grin stayed in place. 'I hope you've entertained yourself with that little fantasy. If what you described had actually happened, why wasn't it uncovered in a police enquiry?'

'Because there never was a proper police enquiry. All they wanted was a headline to bolster their anti-drugs campaign.'

Mo smiled infuriatingly and held out his hands, palms outwards, in a gesture of finality. 'I rest my case,' he said. 'Or I would, if there was a case for me to rest.'

Gerald Tarquin was on his feet, his face suffused with rage. 'You killed Ollie! You killed the only person I have ever loved!'

'It can never be proved that I did.'

The complacency with which these words were spoken only inflamed Gerald Tarquin further. He threw a punch at the scarred face of his tormentor.

That brought Mo to his feet with a quick jab to his opponent's chin. Suddenly, a Sunday afternoon in the sedate Feathers pub in nice middle-class Clincham had turned into a Western bar brawl. The two men grappled and pushed each other back and forth, raining impotent blows, scattering furniture, smashing glasses. Women screamed, children cried, and half-drunk men tried ineffectually to separate the two combatants.

Meanwhile, outside it rained with renewed vigour.

Fortunately, someone behind the bar phoned the police.

The two furious men showed no signs of stopping their fight. Blood streamed down both of their faces as they yelled obscenities at each other. They rose and fell in battle, skidding across the floor, blocking the exits for families desperate to leave. Affronted fathers tried to pull them apart but were only rewarded with bloody noses. The approaching sirens were a welcome sound.

The police did finally manage to separate the two, cuff them and take them off to the station.

Carole, graciously apologetic, said to Jude, 'I got it wrong.'

'I'm pretty sure I got it right,' came the response, 'but how is anyone going to prove it?'

Fortunately, the case against Mo (full name Malcolm Pascoe) was proved. The two men arrested for affray at The Feathers pub were questioned extensively at Clincham Police Station. When asked the reason for their altercation, Gerald Tarquin accused his opponent of the murders of Ollie Luke and Drake Purslow. Though such charges are quite commonly shouted out in drunken brawls, the police thought these deserved investigation.

There had always been a feeling that the death of Ollie Luke had been inadequately dealt with. Though it was some time ago, closed-circuit television footage from The Gryphon Club did confirm the presence of both the victim and Malcolm Pascoe at the relevant time. A Brighton drug dealer, well known to the police, confirmed that Malcolm Pascoe had been an occasional client, and had a record of selling him the relevant drugs, those that were used to inject the fatal overdose, on the Friday before Ollie Luke's death.

The assumption by the police was that Drake Purslow had somehow intimated to Mo that he knew about Ollie Luke's murder and that was why he had to be eliminated.

It took a long time, as such investigations must, but once it was clear the case against the stagehand for killing Ollie Luke was watertight, he confessed to the murder of Drake Purslow, in the hope of reducing his anticipated sentence. And yes, the police had been right in their conjectures about the reason for the second homicide.

For his part in the affray at The Feathers, Gerald Tarquin was given a small fine. But at least his accusations had helped bring to justice the murderer of the only person he had ever loved.

Tony Grover had been too drunk at the time to be aware of what had happened.

NINETEEN

All the legal processes took their usual long time, and when the story of Malcolm Pascoe's conviction was announced, it didn't make much of a splash. The press's memory for television stars is short. And because *House/Home* was thought of as dated and politically incorrect, the series didn't get repeated in the squeaky-clean 2020s. So, the show and everything to do with it was quietly forgotten. A cultural atrocity comparable to Nazi book burnings, as a drunken Tony Grover would bemoan in pubs to anyone prepared to listen.

Katie Clithero shed solitary tears when the truth about her boyfriend's death came out. The news made her even more determined to continue her work against the menace of drugs.

Myrna Crace's prognostication that Johnny Warburton wouldn't leave hospital alive proved all too true. Another stroke, some ten days after Carole and Jude had visited, put paid to him. His funeral was a joyously camp celebration. Never had so many actors done so many gleeful impressions of the same person as they recounted their outrageous Johnny Warburton stories.

And Myrna didn't outlast him by much more than a month. Her funeral was splendidly sedate and brought out all the great and the good of Clincham. She was, after all, Clincham Theatre royalty.

The theatre itself struggled on against dwindling audiences and cuts from arts funding organizations. The winter 'receiving' season remained very uneven, except for sold-out one-night gigs by stand-up comedians which attracted an audience that had never crossed a theatre's threshold before. And the summer 'producing' season constantly tried to do experimental work for a younger demographic, balanced by bland musicals that wouldn't frighten off the older, more traditional playgoers of Clincham.

Fiona Crampton continued to work hard, keeping the shows on the road. And Lazlo, the artistic director, was always off doing another of his lucrative private productions.

Babs Backshaw's fame grew and grew. She went on getting all the fat parts in Hollywood and delighting chat show audiences with tales of her flatulence.

Anita Harcourt continued being a very good shaman (according to the judgement of other shamans and not people like Carole Seddon). Jude kept in touch with her. There were projects on which they could work constructively together.

Imogen Wales had allocated some time to grieving for Drake Purslow after she finished the run of *Coriolanus* at the Duke of York's. But then she was offered Lady Macbeth at the National and got very busy prepping for that. So, her grieving for Drake was postponed indefinitely.

What happened to Gerald Tarquin, no one really knew. He vanished off the radar, and in spite of his devotion to Babs Backshaw, she made no attempt to contact him.

Nell went on guarding the stage door. Nonie went on archiving and doing other volunteer work for Clincham Theatre. And she now had a regular helper who drove over from Fethering twice a week and listened to what she referred to as 'goss' in the Green Room Café.

Jude did observe one evening in the Crown and Anchor, 'I thought you didn't like theatre people, Carole.'

And got the reply, 'Jude, I have no idea what you're talking about.'

Whereupon, Ted Crisp said, 'Will it be two more of those large New Zealand Sauvignon Blancs?'

Which, indeed, it was.

A piece she read in the *Fethering Observer* saddened Jude. It reported the double suicide of an elderly woman called Edith Grant and her daughter Elizabeth.

Heartbreaking, but Jude could understand why. She could even find some admiration for the way Edie must have made the arrangements.

Jude sat in comfort in the back of Linton Braithwaite's car. It was an extravagance to get him to drive her all the way to Wales, but it was an extravagance she felt like indulging.

Sometimes she just had to get out of Fethering.

She had told Carole she'd be away for the weekend but, in spite of a great deal of pressure and wheedling, had not told her neighbour where she was going.

Probably just as well. Carole's reactions would have been all too predictable if she'd been told that Jude was going to join Anita Harcourt for a shamanic retreat in Harlech.